Readers love Andrew Grey

Children of Bacchus

"…a captivating erotic fantasy."
—Romance Junkies

Child of Joy

"…well written and a wonderful treat to read."
—Literary Nymphs

Bottled Up

"…a charming and moving novel."
—Romance Junkies

Love Means… No Shame

"This is one book that will make it to several keeper shelves to be read again and again."
—Literary Nymphs

The Best Revenge

"…this phenomenal story… kept me spell bound from the start."
—Fallen Angel Reviews Recommended Read

http://www.dreamspinnerpress.com

Books by
ANDREW GREY

THE BOTTLED UP STORIES
Bottled Up
Uncorked
The Best Revenge
An Unexpected Vintage

THE CHILDREN OF BACCHUS STORIES
Children of Bacchus
Thursday's Child
Child of Joy

THE LOVE MEANS… STORIES
Love Means… No Shame
Love Means… Courage
Love Means… No Boundaries

All published by
DREAMSPINNER PRESS

AN UNEXPECTED VINTAGE

Andrew Grey

Dreamspinner Press

Published by
Dreamspinner Press
4760 Preston Road
Suite 244-149
Frisco, TX 75034
http://www.dreamspinnerpress.com/

An Unexpected Vintage

Cover Design by Mara McKennen

ISBN: 978-1-61581-403-9

Printed in the United States of America
First Edition
April, 2010

eBook edition available
eBook ISBN: 978-1-61581-404-6

To everyone at The Innocence Project
for all the good work you do.

Chapter 1

GARY got out of his babied, older car and stepped onto the curb, reaching back inside to retrieve the bottle of wine from the passenger seat. Shutting the door, he checked the address on the mailbox and confirmed that he'd found the right house before letting his eyes wander to the front door. His mouth dropped open, and he looked again. This *was* the right place, wasn't it?

He looked up and down the sidewalk and almost got back into his car and drove away. He shouldn't have come. The house was a beautiful Victorian with a turret and meticulously maintained yard. Where he'd been happy a few minutes earlier just to have been invited to a party, his first one in years, now he felt self-conscious about his clothes, which were old, but the nicest he had, and the grocery store bottle of wine he'd brought. Maybe he should just leave and go back to his tiny apartment and drink the entire bottle himself. Life had done a good job of beating him down: a series of jobs that always seemed to evaporate just when he'd get comfortable, and a few boyfriends who turned out to be frogs rather than princes. Unlucky and unremarkable, that was him. As he stood on the sidewalk, he saw the front door open, and he knew it was too late. He'd been seen.

"Gary, come on in." Tyler smiled and waved. "I see you found the place."

Gary forced his feet to move forward and gave himself a quick "what the hell" pep talk. Tyler was a client, a very good client, and he'd invited him to a party at his home. So screwing up his courage, Gary smiled and walked toward the front door.

As soon as he reached the front porch, his hand was clasped in a firm handshake, and he was greeted with a warm smile. "I'm so glad you could make it." Tyler ushered him into the imposing entrance hall with its rich woodwork and impressive furnishings. If Gary hadn't known already, it would be quite obvious from the furnishings that Tyler was a very successful antiques dealer. "Can I take your coat?"

"Thank you." Gary handed Tyler the bottle of wine and then slipped off his fall jacket and handed it to Tyler as well. "I wasn't sure what to bring," he said softly, a little embarrassed at his meager offering.

Tyler smiled brightly, taking the bottle. "You didn't need to bring anything, but thank you." Tyler turned the bottle in his hand looking at the label. "You got one, huh?"

Gary had no idea what Tyler was talking about, and it must have showed on his face.

"Sommelier Wines had already sold out before I could get a bottle," Tyler explained.

"One of what?" Gary asked as he suppressed a smile. He'd obviously gotten lucky with the wine.

"According to Sean, this is one of those unexpected vintages where the bottle costs ten or fifteen bucks and tastes like a hundred dollar bottle of wine. I've been hoping to try this since he sold out." The smile stayed in place as Tyler went on to explain, "Drinks are in the kitchen, food's in the dining room. Please make yourself comfortable."

Gary followed Tyler through to the kitchen where a large assortment of wine, liquor, and mixers were set out. A small crowd was standing near the bar, and a handsome older man was mixing drinks. "What would you like?" he asked as he looked at Gary.

"I'm not sure." He never knew what to order. Most people thought what he liked was too fruity. "What seems to be popular?"

"I have a pitcher of daiquiris if you'd like one, white and red wine, or I can mix you a cocktail. Just name your poison." The man smiled, and Gary realized that for an older man, he was a real hunk.

Gary watched as another older hunk approached and slipped his arm around the bartender's waist.

"A daiquiri would be nice, thank you." Gary watched as his drink was poured and handed to him.

"By the way, I'm Bill Janssens, and this is my partner, Tom Carter." He held out his hand.

"Gary Keller." He shook both men's hands and smiled nervously.

"How do you know Tyler and Mark, Gary?" Bill poured himself a drink and stepped from behind the counter-slash-bar, Tom's arm still around his waist.

"I'm the Milwaukee representative for Gregory Martin Fabrics, and Tyler uses a lot of my fabrics when he reupholsters the antiques for the store." He took a sip of his drink, pulling his eyes momentarily away from the attractive men.

"Do you sell to individuals?" Tom asked, as Bill kissed him softly and then moved away.

"No, I'm a wholesaler, but anything you need could be gotten through Tyler." Gary took another sip and felt the alcohol start to warm his stomach. God, this was strong stuff.

"I need new curtains for the house. I made the last ones years ago, but I just don't have the time anymore."

Gary reached into his back pocket and pulled out a business card. "Give me a call, and I could meet you at Tyler's if he's willing. I've got a car full of books, and we make all different styles of curtains and draperies."

Tom raised his glass a little. "Gary, you're a lifesaver. I'll call you next week and set something up. I'm sure Tyler won't have a problem." Gary saw Bill motioning for Tom, and Gary expected him to move away, but Tom seemed to pull Gary along with him as he joined his partner, entering a circle of people who obviously knew each other.

"Gary, this is Sean and Sam, and their son Bobby and his partner Kenny." Gary shook hands with each of them.

"Haven't I seen you at Tyler's?" Bobby smiled as he took a gulp of his beer.

"I've seen you a few times. You're usually working with Mark. You're an artist, right?"

"Yeah. Mark and I are working on a project together." Bobby was obviously proud and pleased to be working with Mark.

"Tom, we were just talking about the cruise next month, and Sean told me that Phillip needs a roommate. He had one but the guy backed out because of a family issue, and now he's stuck." Bill looked truly disappointed for his friend.

"A cruise, wow. Where are you going?" Gary let his excitement overrule his usual reticence.

"We leave out of Puerto Rico and stop in Barbados, Antigua, St. Croix, St. Maarten, and St. Lucia. It should be a lot of fun," Tom said, with a little excitement of his own.

Gary looked at Bobby and Kenny. "Are you going too?" He sipped the strong drink, careful not to overdo it on an empty stomach.

Kenny answered for the two of them. "Bobby's watching the antique store for Tyler and I'm watching the wine store for Sean."

Tom set his empty glass on a coaster. "Is Phillip going to be here tonight?"

"Tyler told me he'd been invited." Sean looked around the room. "Speak of the devil." A tall, handsome, blond man in his early thirties approached the group. Hugs were exchanged and introductions made.

"I understand you don't have a roommate for the cruise," Tom commented.

"Yeah, Craig backed out at the last minute. I can't blame him, though. His mother's having health issues, and he can't be away for too long. Cost him enough, anyway. He'd already paid for half the cruise and they won't refund it. So he's out that, but if I still want to go, I have to pay for my passage plus the other half of his."

"When's the deadline?" Tyler asked as he joined the group.

"The travel agent said I have to let her know by Monday. I figure I'll go and pay the extra, but I'd be able to do more on the islands if a roommate freed up the extra cash, you know?"

"Gary, why don't you go?" Tyler asked, and all heads in the group turned to him.

Gary didn't know what to say or how to react. He'd love to go on a cruise—he hadn't had a vacation in at least two years, but he wasn't sure he had the money to spare, and he'd be rooming with a complete stranger. "I don't know if I can afford it," he said softly, regretting the words as soon as they crossed his lips.

"It's not very expensive," Phillip supplied, looking a little excited. And Gary had to admit, as he looked into those deep blue eyes, he wouldn't mind sharing a room for a week with a guy like that. He could feel heat settle in his groin, and he had to force his mind back to the topic at hand and off his starved libido. "Craig already paid for half the fare. So you'd just need to pay the other half and the airfare. The food's included on the ship."

Gary thought about it. It sounded like a lot of fun and maybe it wouldn't cost too much. He'd been working hard for years, making ends meet and making do. He deserved a little excitement and some fun. November was a slow month for him anyway, and so far October had been pretty good. "Can I think about it?"

Phillip beamed back at him, and he almost said he'd go just to see that smile again. "Sure, would you like to meet for lunch tomorrow? We could get to know each other, and I could go over things with you." Gary found himself agreeing before he could think twice about it.

Gary saw Tyler smile as he stepped away from the group. He followed, looking at all the incredible works of art as Tyler wandered through the house making sure his guests were happy. Gary noticed that Tyler kept checking his watch. "Where are you, Mark?" he heard Tyler whisper as he peeked out the front window from the office. Gary was about to go to him, until he saw Bill coming over.

"Is something wrong?"

Startled, Tyler jumped a little as Bill approached.

"No. I'm just wondering what's keeping Mark." He'd been doing that a lot lately. Tyler turned away from the window and faced his close friend.

"Is there something wrong?" Bill asked, obviously concerned for his friend.

"I don't want to think there is, but I'm really starting to wonder." The patter of scampering feet on the wood interrupted them as a miniature dachshund began jumping around Tyler's leg. He picked her up and she kissed him before settling in his arms. "We used to go into the store together most mornings, and when the store closed, we'd ride home together. Now Mark sleeps in, gets to his studio at noon, and doesn't leave till late. He never says what he's doing, and when I ask, he's evasive."

"You think Mark's having an affair?" Bill's tone said that he didn't believe it. "Mark loves you more than life itself. You know that. There's no way he'd have an affair."

"Then what other explanation is there?"

"Lots. Thousands. Maybe he's just working."

Tyler set down the dog down, and she scampered around the room, doing a doggie vacuum cleaner routine. Then she jumped around Gary's legs looking for attention. Sitting in one of the hall chairs, he picked her up and set her on his lap. Tyler's voice carried to where he was sitting, but he didn't mean to overhear. "I've checked his studio a few times, and I can't see anything that would take up that kind of time."

"There's an explanation Tyler. You just have to trust him."

"I do trust him; that's what's beginning to hurt. I hate this feeling of helplessness and doubt. Mark's my whole world, and if anything ever happened to him, to us, I don't know what I'd do. I just don't know how to deal with this." Gary saw the front door open, and the dog jumped down from his lap, running across the hall, jumping around Mark's legs.

"Jolie, how's my girl?" Mark looked so happy to be home.

"Talk to him, Tyler. Tell him how you feel." The words drifted from the office, and Bill walked out of the office door, Gary watching him head toward the back of the house. Mark walked into the office, carrying Jolie.

"I'm sorry, Ty. I got caught up and lost track of time." Gary got up from the chair and walked in front of the open office door. He saw Mark kiss Tyler and then put Jolie down before kissing Tyler again, hard. Tyler almost backed away in surprise, but returned the kiss, his passion for this man evident.

"I'm sorry I've been so tired lately," Mark said softly.

Gary turned away to leave them alone. It sounded like they needed the privacy. He hoped there wasn't something going on. Gary really liked Tyler, and he'd seen him and Mark together for as long as Tyler had been a client. They were an inspiration to him. Whatever was wrong, he hoped they worked it out.

"We should join our guests." Tyler began to walk toward the door, but he felt Mark's tug at his arm.

"They'll wait a few minutes."

Gary couldn't help turning around. The two of them were so loving to each other. He watched Mark pull Tyler to him and kiss him again as Jolie bounded around their feet. "Once this is over, I intend to take you upstairs and make up for all the time I haven't been around lately. I love you, Ty."

Gary turned away and left the room, not wanting to tempt himself to watch any more. It wasn't right, but what he'd seen warmed his heart. He wanted that so badly: someone to love who would love him back, someone who actually saw him. And Gary thought, not for the first time, that maybe that was the problem. Gary walked through the magnificent house and wandered into what he guessed was the family room, where he saw Bill and Sean talking together in the corner.

"I hope things are okay with them." The concern on Bill's face was plainly evident. "I did notice as I left that Mark gave Tyler quite a lip-lock. I hope he's mistaken."

"I'm sure he is," Sean said, as Gary made his way to them, hoping they'd welcome him into their conversation.

"Does Tom know?" Sean asked, obviously being cagey.

Bill turned, staring into Sean's eyes. "No, he has no idea at all." Bill smiled conspiratorially. "Can we meet this week? I really need to make sure everything is absolutely perfect."

"It will be, don't worry. Tom will never see this coming." Sean sipped his wine and returned Bill's look as Gary stood next to them.

"See what coming?" Tom asked.

Gary saw Tom's arms slip around Bill's waist as he nuzzled Bill's neck and ear. He loved that they weren't afraid to demonstrate their love for one another.

"Nothing." Bill looked momentarily flustered and then recovered, like he'd been caught doing something he shouldn't. "We were just trying to decide which excursions we might like to take during the cruise. There's a snorkeling package on Barbados with a catamaran that includes the chance to snorkel in Turtle Bay. The guide says we may even see some sea turtles. Sean was telling me that without your glasses, one could come up right behind you and you'd never see it coming."

Gary knew that wasn't at all what they'd been saying. It had sounded to him like they were planning some sort of surprise for Tom, and he didn't want to spoil it. Tom didn't look like he was buying it, but then Bill began pressing back against Tom, and Gary almost laughed at the far-away, lustful look that passed over Tom's face. Gary noticed that the subject died, just like Bill was probably hoping it would.

"If you'll excuse me, I need to see what Sam is up to." Sean made a hasty retreat, and Gary retrieved his drink from the table, intending to follow.

"Bill, what are you up to?" Gary saw Tom's hand graze over Bill's pants. "Plenty, I guess."

Gary hastened his retreat. He was starting to feel like a voyeur, and it was making him a little uncomfortable. Bill turned in Tom's embrace. "We're at a party, remember?" The rest of what was said faded away as Gary left them alone in the room and headed to the dining room, where Phillip was filling a plate. Gary joined him and Phillip smiled and began talking. Gary made up a plate and followed Phillip into the living room, where they sat down and talked… and talked. It had been a long time since he'd sat down and really talked to someone, and it felt good.

As the evening wore on, people began getting their coats and leaving. Gary got up from the chair he'd occupied for the last few hours. "I should get going as well."

Phillip stood up and, to Gary's surprise, gave him a hug. "I'll see you for lunch tomorrow. I hope you decide to go on the cruise. We'll have so much fun." Phillip hugged him again, and Gary found he was really looking forward to that lunch.

Chapter 2

GARY smiled to himself as he lay in his warm bed, the sun trying its feeble best to shine through his small bedroom window—not that he ever got any real sunshine, let alone much light, through the window overlooking a small courtyard between the crowded buildings. The quirky apartment in the old building was small, clean, and nice, but far from luxurious. Gary yawned and resettled under the covers. It was early, and he was still a little tired from last night. The party had been a lot of fun, and he'd even noticed that some of the couples had looked like they were ready to sneak off together. What surprised him was that it was the older couple, Tom and Bill, who seemed the most likely to be caught having sex among the coats. Man, they were a sexy pair.

Thinking of sexy, Gary's mind flashed to an image of Phillip, and what an image it was. His clothing at the party had hinted at strong arms and powerful legs. His broad shoulders, big blue eyes, and waves of blond hair had captured Gary's attention for most of the evening. Shaking his head, Gary forced the vision away. Getting out of the warm blankets, he trudged to the tiny bathroom, shaved, and brushed his teeth before starting the shower.

Stepping under the warm spray, the image of Phillip returned. His hand slid down his stomach as the vision of Phillip from the party morphed into a vision of what Phillip would look like naked. Now, that was sexy: long, powerful legs, strong chest with big nipples he could suck on. Gary's hand began stroking as his fantasy continued. Letting his mind have free rein, he wondered what Phillip's skin would taste like, what it would be like to kiss him and touch him, and what his butt would feel like as his palm slipped over the swell and his fingers dipped—

Gary's fantasy ended wonderfully as his climax barreled into him. His head tingled, and his body shook as he came hard, spilling himself on his hands and into the tub, the water washing everything away. He let himself catch his breath, and the vision faded slowly as he began washing his hair.

Clean and still wonderfully mellow, Gary dried himself and walked naked into his bedroom. Dressing quickly so he wouldn't get cold, he checked the clock and realized he'd slept later than normal. Speeding up the pace, he pulled on his socks and shoes before grabbing his coat and leaving the apartment for his lunch with the object of his fantasy.

It didn't take him long to get to the deli. Pulling open the door, he saw Phillip right away. He waved and smiled as Gary walked to the table. "Have you been here long?"

Phillip shook his head. "Just got here a few minutes ago." He motioned to the other chair, and Gary sat down as a young man about his age came over to the table and took their orders. "I brought the cruise information." He pulled up a messenger bag and retrieved a small manila envelope. "This has all the information about the cruise, and I have the cost information here." He pulled out his receipt for the cruise. "Craig already paid for half the cruise. I talked to the travel agent, and they said they can transfer the reservation as long as they do it Monday."

Gary listened to Phillip's voice and watched those incredible eyes as he talked. "It should cost you about a thousand dollars for the airfare and the rest of the cost of the cruise." Their food arrived, and Phillip set the papers aside as they started eating.

"So what do you do?" Gary asked as he took a bite of his turkey croissant.

"I design furniture."

Gary's excitement bubbled over. "That's so cool. Do you have any of your designs?" Gary put down his sandwich and looked at Phillip expectantly, wondering why he hadn't asked that question the night before. They'd talked about so many things but not about work.

"They're in my bag." Putting down his own sandwich, Phillip wiped his fingers and then pulled a schematic drawing out of his bag. "I'm trying to find someone interested in bringing them to life."

Gary took the drawing and looked at it carefully. "This is great. I can see myself sitting in this chair, and I love the swoop of the arm. It's so dramatic, and yet, I bet it's really comfortable. Are you able to do this for a living?"

"No. This is my hobby, but it's what I really want to do. I work as a draftsman for an architectural firm to pay the bills, but this is my passion." A light shone in Phillip's eyes and Gary found it the sexiest thing he'd ever seen, and he wondered what it would be like to have some of that passion directed at him.

Gary felt his hand start to shake slightly as he looked at the rest of the drawings, flipping the pages one after the other. The amazing thing was that for each design, he could see one of his fabrics on the piece, complementing the design. "Could you get me copies of these? My company has a furniture line that they're just starting, and I'd like to pass these designs to them." He looked up and saw the delight on Phillip's face. "I can't make promises, but I will definitely pass them to the proper people." He handed the drawings back to Phillip, who put them back in his bag.

"Hell yes!" His smile was huge and bright.

Gary basked in it as he picked up his sandwich. "So do you really think you'd like me as your roommate for a week?"

"You mean you'll come?" Gary nodded, and Phillip's grin was infectious.

"It sounds like a lot of fun. Have you been on one of these before?"

Phillip shook his head as he swallowed. "No. But Sean and Sam have, and they loved it. They told me to bring plenty of sunblock, shorts, tank tops, and bathing suits. They also said that we need to dress up two nights at dinner, but the other nights are sporty casual."

Gary found himself getting excited. "Should I call the travel agent?" He finished the last bite of his lunch and finished drinking his soda.

Phillip swallowed before answering. "I'll call her in the morning and have her call you."

Gary fished into his wallet and handed Phillip one of his business cards. "Have her call the cell."

Phillip took the card and put it in his wallet, picking up the check as the server placed it on the table. Gary started to object, but Phillip wouldn't hear of it. "This is my treat." Gary watched as Phillip got up to pay. Tight jeans hugged a full butt below the small waist and broad shoulders he'd noticed the night before. But today was different—today Gary could see that the tall blond was everything he'd imagined and probably more. "I was wondering if you'd like to come back to my place and hang out for a while."

Today was the one day Gary allowed himself off each week, and having someone to spend part of it with sounded really nice. "Sure, that'd be great."

"I'm just down the street in the Prospect Arms."

"That's the building next to mine. I'm in the Terrace."

"Apartment 1215. Give me a few minutes to make things presentable, and I'll meet you there in ten." Phillip picked up his bag and left the deli, walking briskly down the sidewalk. Gary watched for a minute and then pulled on his jacket before leaving the deli himself and hurrying to his own building.

In the lobby he pressed the button and cursed the slow elevator. When the doors finally opened, he hurried inside and pressed the button for the fourth floor. The doors closed, and he willed the thing to move faster, hurrying out again as soon as the doors parted and almost bumping into Mrs. Hueners as she carried out her trash. Calling his apologies he hurried inside. Dropping his bag on the sofa, he hurried to the bathroom and tried to make himself as presentable as possible.

Five minutes later he was rushing back to the elevator in a fresh shirt, carrying his jacket. This time he didn't nearly run over anyone, and he shortly found himself outside Phillip's door. He knocked, and the door opened to Phillip's bright smile.

"I hope you like beer." Gary held up the six-pack he'd pulled from the refrigerator just before he left the apartment. There was no way he could show up empty-handed, even if it meant he'd had to bring the last of his beer.

Taking the offerings, Phillip ushered him inside. The apartment was nothing like Gary's. It had a huge living room, big, bright windows, and a sliding door that opened onto a large patio area. "This is a great apartment."

"Thanks. They renovated the building a few years ago, and the architectural firm I worked for handled the design. The lucky thing was that this unit became available during the renovations, and I was able to get it. There are only four like it in the building."

Phillip turned on the huge television. Gary sat on the sofa while Phillip brought bowls of chips and pretzels, popping open a couple of the beers that Gary had brought. "Do you like football? Green Bay's playing." Phillip changed the channel and the television switched from the Cooking Channel, which Gary would have preferred, to ESPN. Then Phillip settled on the sofa next to him, and Gary really didn't care what was on the television. Phillip's warm scent and light cologne wafted into his nose, and he reclined back on the comfortable cushions, doing his best to watch the game. At halftime Green Bay was ahead by twelve points. It really looked like a blowout in the making.

Gary thought Phillip was getting closer. Turning to check he found himself looking directly into Phillip's eyes, and he did indeed seem to be getting closer and closer. Then he felt a firm hand on the back of his head drawing them together. When Phillip kissed him, it was firm and hot, nearly curling his toes. The kiss deepened and became more forceful, powerful. Phillip shifted on the sofa, pressing him into the cushions as his tongue devoured Gary's mouth. He felt Phillip's hands slide beneath his shirt, fingers zeroing in on his nipples, plucking them softly at first and then a little harder.

Gary found himself moaning softly and arched into the touch. It had been a while since anyone had touched him this way, and it hadn't been like this, like he was being devoured. Gary found himself holding onto Phillip's back, trying to hang on as Phillip played his body like an instrument.

"You're so responsive," Phillip said softly as the broke their kiss. "Would you like to move this to the bedroom?" All Gary could do was nod as he felt Phillip's weight lift off him. Then his hand was taken, and Phillip led him to the bedroom.

The room was masculine, with a substantial bed and richly colored bedding set off against neutral walls. Gary glanced around and then felt Phillip drawing him close, kissing him again. This time, as those lips pulled at his, he felt Phillip's hands on his shirt, drawing it up and then pulling it off, the kiss breaking only long enough to slip the shirt over his head. His pants opened, almost on their own, and he felt Phillip's hands slide down his back, pushing the fabric over his butt until his pants slid down his legs. Gary toed off his shoes and stepped out of his pants, standing naked as Phillip stepped back.

Gary could almost feel Phillip's gaze as it raked over him, taking him in from head to toe. His first instinct was to try to hide; he knew he wasn't a stunning beauty.

"Very nice." Phillip's eyes kept roving.

Gary knew now that Phillip was being charitable. "I am not. I'm skinny and pasty." He was becoming very self-conscious, but when he looked at Phillip's face he saw something he'd never seen before: want. And before Gary could move, Phillip had him pulled against him and was kissing him again. Then he felt himself being pressed back against the bed.

"Do I make you feel skinny and pasty as you say, or do I make you feel sexy?" If Phillip kept kissing him like that, he could have anything he wanted. When Gary didn't answer, Phillip began sucking the base of his neck. "I thought so. You taste sexy and hot, you know that?" Gary answered with a shake of his head. "Well, you do."

Gary's body was starving for Phillip's touch, but he was only given kisses and caresses that never went lower than his shoulders. He arched his back against him, but Phillip wasn't having any of it.

"Just relax. I'll take care of you, but you need to show some patience." Then the lips and touch were gone.

Gary opened his eyes and saw Phillip standing at the foot of the bed. Slowly he opened the buttons of his shirt, parting the fabric before slipping it off his arms and to the floor. Gary took in the strong chest and tight stomach, then noticed the full nipples with silver bars through them. "Didn't that hurt?"

"Maybe at first, but what's a little pain when it brings so much pleasure later?" Phillip began opening his pants and any other questions flew from Gary's mind as the jeans slid down Phillip's legs, his briefs following close behind. His penis was big and standing proud, with a silver ring through the head. "Before you ask, yes it did."

Gary had never seen a pierced dick before, except maybe once in a porno, and he found he couldn't take his eyes off it. And it wasn't just the jewelry—it was everything about the man, even better than his fantasy. "Wow," was the most articulate thing he could come up with.

Phillip climbed back on the bed and on top of Gary, their skin sliding together. "What do you like, Gary?" He wasn't sure how to answer that question. He wasn't into anything special, and he definitely wasn't kinky or anything, but it seemed as though maybe Phillip was. To his relief Phillip interpreted his silence correctly. "I promise we won't do anything you're not comfortable with."

Gary nodded, and Phillip began kissing him again, but this time as he did, Gary ran his hands down Phillip's powerful back, the muscles rippling beneath his hands. Suddenly they rolled on the bed, and Gary found himself looking down into Phillip's blue eyes. He kissed the man's lips, then lowered his head, capturing a nipple between his lips. The bars felt cool against the hot skin as he played with them, his tongue sliding around the tiny spheres that capped the ends. Moving to the other, he sucked the bud to a hard point, twisting the bar with his teeth.

Phillip let go, loudly moaning, "Fuck, Gary, that's good." He'd almost stopped, but Phillip seemed to enjoy it, so he kept it up as his hands wandered over the smooth skin covered with hard muscle.

Figuring he'd see what else Phillip liked, he slid down his body, fingers fastening onto the bars, continuing to work the nipples as he slid his tongue around the head of Phillip's cock and over the heavy ring. Phillip released another groan and bucked his hips.

"Now who's getting impatient?" Gary smirked as he took more of Phillip into his mouth. The ring initially felt cool as it slid over his tongue. It was different and a curiosity, but it didn't really turn him on. Phillip, on the other hand, went crazy when Gary tugged on the ring with his tongue.

"Gary, can I fuck you?" Between heaving breaths, Phillip huffed, "I really need to be inside you."

As an answer Gary let Phillip slip from between his lips. "How do you want me?"

Phillip pulled Gary to him and kissed him hard. "Lie on your stomach."

He was big, and Gary felt relieved, knowing this would be the easiest way for him to take him. Palms stroked his back, and he felt lips kiss his skin. The hands slid to his butt, massaging his cheeks and pulling them apart. Gary twisted to see as he felt warm air against him, and then a hot tongue slid down his crease. "Phillip," he cried out as the tongue speared his opening. He'd never felt anything like that before in his life. He stretched his legs open farther, hoping that Phillip would understand. He did, chuckling softly before tongue-fucking him again and again, until Gary thought he would turn to JELL-O. A finger joined the tongue, teasing the skin before sliding inside.

Gary jumped as Phillip found the happy spot and sent a jolt through him. He felt a stretch as Phillip added a second finger and then a third.

The bed shifted. He heard a wrapper tear open, and then Phillip was pressing into him. He felt the ring slip into him. The stretch and burn were intense as Phillip breached him and then slid home. Gary could barely breathe as Phillip slid in deep in a single, fluid movement. His back arched on its own, and he felt Phillip's hand hold his chest as he began to move deep inside him, slowly at first, and then building speed. Phillip felt good, and Gary had never been so full in his life, but he didn't feel connected to him, not the way he thought he would with that special person. As the intensity built, all thoughts flew from his head, and Gary went with it, bucking against Phillip's thrusts, sweat bursting out all over his body as he felt the pressure build. Each thrust reverberated through Gary's body, rubbing him against the sheets, and each movement brought him closer to the edge. He felt Phillip's rhythm become erratic. Gary's mind clouded, and he came in buckets against the bedding as Phillip groaned loudly and stilled, throbbing deep inside him. Then a weight pressed him into the mattress as Phillip collapsed.

Both of them caught their breath, and Phillip began kissing his shoulder as he slipped from his body and rolled onto the mattress, pulling Gary into his arms. "You were wonderful."

"So were you." Gary returned Phillip's tenderness as he felt his eyelids begin to close. Lying there in Phillip's arms, he felt so comfortable he soon nodded off.

When he woke, Phillip was still holding him. He, too, had drifted off. Gary wasn't sure what Phillip would want. As he began to shift, he saw Phillip's blue eyes flutter open, and he smiled at him. "Are you okay?"

"I'm fine, Phillip." The sex had been great, probably the best he'd ever had, but he hadn't felt that connection with him, and he didn't know how to tell him.

"You seem kind of tense."

"Well, you were incredible, but...." He couldn't bring himself to say it. He didn't want to hurt Phillip's feelings any more than he'd want his feelings hurt, but he knew he'd want to know the truth.

Phillip began to chuckle. "It's okay, you can say it."

"I just didn't feel that spark, that connection, you know?"

"It's okay, Gary. We had a good time. It certainly doesn't mean you have to marry me or anything. And just for the record, you're a great guy, and you're going to make someone very happy, but I don't think you're what I need, either."

"I'm not?"

Phillip got out of bed and opened his closet, showing Gary all the leather hanging behind the door. "I think I need someone a little kinkier."

Gary began to laugh as well as he looked at the straps and harnesses. Hell, he didn't know what most of that stuff was, let alone want it used on him. "I'd say so, although the pierced dick should have been my first clue." Gary got out of bed and began picking up his clothes, feeling a little embarrassed again. "Does that mean you still want me as your roommate on the cruise? I'll understand if you don't."

He felt Phillip's arms around him and a set of knuckles ran over his head, giving him a noogie. "Of course I do. We're going to have a lot of fun. Fuck, I think we'll end up being good friends. After all, the hard part's over—I've already seen you naked." Phillip began pulling on his clothes as well. "Come on, let see what else is on TV. We've still got beer to finish." After pulling on their clothes, Phillip grabbed him around the shoulders, and they sat together comfortably on the sofa watching football.

Chapter 3

"THAT might work," Tyler commented as he leafed through a book of upholstery fabric. "I need something rich looking but plain enough that it'll be appealing to a number of people."

Gary turned to the stack of books he'd brought and began searching. "I have this one. It's got mostly solid colors with various textures." He handed the book to Tyler, who began leafing through the samples.

"I wish I'd known about you months ago," Tom piped in as he looked through drapery fabric samples. "We've been to every store in town and could never find anything." Tom had set a number of books aside, samples marked with pieces of paper for later consideration.

Gary noticed that Tom kept looking over at Tyler with a concerned look on his face, like he was wondering if it was okay for him to ask something.

"Are things okay with you and Mark?" Tom finally asked.

Tyler looked like he was pretending he hadn't heard the question, but it seemed as if Tom wasn't going to accept silence as an answer. "I don't know. I wish I did." Gary stopped fussing with the books, and Tom stopped what he was doing, his hand on the last sample he'd looked at. "He started keeping weird hours about three months ago, and he started getting evasive and secretive. After the party he was back to his old self, and I thought I was just imagining things, but about ten days ago, he got even more secretive, and now I barely see him at all, except when he falls into bed exhausted."

"Has he ever done this before?" Gary asked, concerned for his friend.

Tyler shook his head. "No. For almost seven years, we've had a great relationship, and all of a sudden, it seems like I'm on the outside looking in, wondering what the hell happened." Tyler began looking through the book again, but he obviously wasn't seeing anything, and Gary gently took the book away, holding his place for him.

"Have you asked him about it?"

"I did a few days ago. He asked me to trust him. That night he came home early and spent the entire evening at home, but since then he's been back to the same schedule. I don't want to believe it, but I'm seriously starting to think he's having an affair." Tyler held up his hand as they both started to speak together. "I know in my heart that Mark would never do that, and I'm trying desperately not to jump to that conclusion. But the other night, as I was closing up, I heard the back door open and close. When I asked Mark about it, he played dumb and almost accused me of hearing things. Then he went back to work, and I heard him lock the studio door."

"Maybe he's working on some secret project or something," Gary offered, trying to give some sort of logical explanation.

"He's never kept his work from me before. Why start now?" Tyler took a deep breath and slowly released it. "Let's get back to this—we don't need to spend all day talking about my problems." Tyler took the book back from Gary and began looking through it again.

Gary didn't know what to say, and it seemed as though Tom didn't either, because they all remained quiet. "It's okay, guys. There's probably an explanation, and Mark will tell me when he's ready." Gary knew Tyler was putting his best face on things for their sake, and he changed the subject. "Are you ready for the cruise?"

Tom smiled. "I swear Bill's already got his suitcase packed and half of mine as well. I understand there's a costume party one of the nights, and Bill's decided he wants to go for something shocking."

Gary was afraid to ask, but Tyler had no such issues. "How shocking are we talking?"

Tom smirked knowingly. "I've been sworn to secrecy, but be prepared. I figure at least three of the old ladies on the ship will probably swoon."

The bell on the front door jingled, and Tyler got up to greet the customer, spending a few minutes helping the lady and showing her around the store.

Tom seemed happy, but Gary was suddenly worried. He'd spent the last two weeks figuring out what he was going to take to make sure he didn't look too shabby. So many of his clothes were older, and he didn't want to embarrass himself. The last few years had been pretty rough financially. He'd gotten this job just a year earlier, and while he was doing fairly well, his pay was strictly commission, so he was careful to live well within his means. His only extravagance was the cruise he was taking with his friends. And now he had to come up with a costume. "What sort of costume do we need?"

Tom looked him over and smiled. "If you don't have anything, I think I have something you could borrow."

"Thanks, I'd appreciate it."

"No problem."

Tom set his book aside and began reviewing his selections. "Tyler told me you haven't been in town all that long. Do you like it?"

"Yeah, I really do. There's so much to do." He'd begun to like it more, particularly in the last month. "I moved here a year ago when I got this job. The hardest thing is meeting people." He pointed to a particular fabric in the book Tom was holding. "I thought this one would work in your living room." They'd had him over for dinner a few days earlier, so Gary had seen their house and knew pretty well what would work for them and their style.

Tyler seemed to settle on his selection and placed his order. Tom still had final decisions to make. "Let me order you samples of these fabrics. I can have them shipped directly to you. Once you've decided just give them back to me." Tom agreed, and Gary wrote down the numbers and called in both the order and the request for samples.

Tom said his good-byes and, after hugging them both, left the store. Gary picked up the books as the front door chimed again indicating that Tyler had more customers. Gary said a quick good-bye, packing everything into the trunk of his car. He saw Tyler through the store windows and waved as he climbed into the car and headed toward his next appointment.

He only had to travel a few blocks before pulling up in front of an interior design studio. This was one of the accounts he'd inherited with the territory, and they hadn't been providing much business for him. Gary was hoping that he could rectify that. Parking in front, he straightened his tie and got out of the car, taking his attaché case with him. The shop looked beautiful, with fantastic window displays and soft muted colors, but as soon as he opened the door, he realized that calm beauty was deceiving.

People were yelling and rushing around. Gary tried to stop someone, but they kept moving. "Can I help you?" The affected speech almost made Gary laugh.

Gary looked at the impeccably dressed older man with gray hair. "I'm Gary Keller with Gregory Martin Fabrics. I have an appointment with Fabrizio."

"Of course." The man practically swished to him, holding out a hand. "I'm Fabrizio Gionconna. It's a pleasure to meet you." He looked around the shop and seemed to notice the pandemonium for the first time. "We're getting ready for the design show, and it's been a madhouse."

"I understand, and I won't take up much of your time. I wanted to stop by and see what I could do for you."

He shook his head in a very dramatic way and pointed to a few books stacked in a corner. "I just don't know. I show your stuff, and my customers just aren't interested."

Gary went to the books and began looking through them. "When was the last time a rep came to visit you?"

He began flouncing again, making a show of trying to remember. "I believe it was an adorable man with a mustache?"

"Karl?"

"Yeah, that's it."

Karl was at least two reps ago—no wonder he hadn't done much business. The books they had were years old and completely useless. "I'll be right back." Gary went to his trunk and got a fresh box of basic designer books, hauling them into the store.

"You used to do very well, but your books are years out of date." Gary set the old books aside and opened the box of current offerings. Pulling out one of the books, he opened it and showed it to Fabrizio. "Does this look better?"

The man smiled. "Better? Those look divine." Fabrizio grabbed the book and began thumbing through it as he walked toward the back room, motioning Gary to follow. "I've been looking for the perfect chintz for that chair for two months, and in you walk." Pointing to a swatch of fabric in the book, Fabrizio said, "And there it is." He held the fabric to the chair and stepped back. "It's perfect, and it even runs the right way. I need ten yards as fast as you can get it here."

"Let me make a call." Gary stepped away and dialed the order desk. "They have it in stock, and the cutoff is an hour away."

"Can I get it tomorrow?" Gary relayed the request and nodded affirmatively to Fabrizio. "Then order it."

Gary got all the pertinent account information and completed the order before thanking the representative and hanging up the phone. Fabrizio was already telling the ladies in the shop about the fabric he had coming and what they were going to need to do.

"It should arrive in the morning by FedEx," Gary said.

Fabrizio went back to looking through the books, showing them to one of the ladies while Gary hauled away the old books and got the new ones settled in a good location in the display. This was what he liked about his job. It had taken time for him to get to the smaller producers because the territory had been such a mess, but he kept finding some that he realized could be gems if they were given the right tools and help.

"Can I call you if I need something?"

Gary handed Fabrizio a card. "Call any time. My number is also behind the front cover of all the books." Fabrizio put the book he'd been looking at with the others.

"Thank you. I'd given up hope and was about to just throw those old things away." He indicated the outdated books with a swish of his hand. "I don't mean to be rude, but I have to get back." He leaned forward and kissed Gary on both cheeks, patting his bottom. "Don't be a stranger, honey." Gary smiled and nearly laughed as he left the shop and went to his car. He'd made a good sale and gotten some potential future business. Not bad for an account his manager had told him was probably dead. Getting in the car, he pulled away and headed to his next account.

The rest of his day was productive, and he was about to pack it in when his phone rang. Tyler's order had been shipped and was expected to arrive in a few days. Since he was in that area of town, he decided he'd stop by on the off chance that Tyler was still there.

The front of the store looked dark—Tyler's store was obviously closed. Pulling into a parking space, he pulled out his phone and dialed the number to leave a message. As he watched, a man approached the front of the store, looking around. Gary thought it strange and watched, thinking he might try to break in or something. As he watched, the front door of the store opened, and Gary saw Mark usher the man inside, closing the door behind them.

He hadn't been paying attention and, hearing a beep, he realized Tyler's answering machine had already played its message, so he left Tyler the details about the order and hung up. Then he looked down and began punching numbers. "Phillip, are you at home? Can I stop by? I have to ask you something."

"Of course. I was about to get dinner, but we could order a pizza."

"Great, I'll see you in a few minutes." Gary pulled away and drove home, parking in the only available space he could find. He had to walk a block or so to get to Phillip's building. At his apartment door, Gary knocked, and Phillip ushered him inside. "The pizza should be here in twenty minutes. So what's the big emergency?"

Gary explained about his conversation with Tyler and what he'd seen at the store. "Should I say something?"

"Good God, no. What you saw could be completely innocent, and you'd be causing him pain for nothing."

"But if it were me, I'd want to know."

"But you don't know anything. Tyler's afraid Mark may be having an affair, and you see Mark letting a man into the store. If I were having an affair, I'd certainly want to do it in the back room of an antique store." Phillip smiled. "It's probably innocent, with a completely logical explanation."

"Maybe." Gary wasn't really convinced.

"Mark and Tyler are the greatest couple I've ever met. If you saw a man going into the store, then Mark has a very good reason. The last thing he'd ever do is cheat on Tyler."

"But…."

Phillip leaned forward. "Gary, Mark is not having an affair."

"How do you know?" Gary looked into his friend's eyes, watching him closely.

"I just do."

Gary got the sneaking suspicion that Phillip knew more than he was telling, but the bell rang telling them that the pizza had arrived, and Phillip left the apartment, returning a few minutes later. With the television on and the pizza before them, their conversation moved on to other things.

Chapter 4

THE past few weeks had been extraordinary for Gary. He and Phillip had gotten together at least twice a week, and they'd had a lot of fun doing guy things together. They hadn't had sex again, and that was fine. He liked having a new friend, a fun friend, and over the last month, he seemed to have acquired a number of those. He'd had dinner at Sean and Sam's, and at Tom and Bill's. He and Phillip had even had the entire group to Phillip's apartment for dinner. Gary had cooked, and Phillip had provided the place. Gary had wanted to reciprocate his new friends' invitations, but his apartment was too small and, in his mind, wasn't good enough. Phillip had offered his apartment for a joint dinner party, and Gary had gratefully accepted. They'd used those opportunities to plan the cruise and talk over detailed arrangements.

He'd also had a great month businesswise. Tyler had placed a large order for fabric that included all of Tom and Bill's new curtains for their home. And a number of the designers he'd visited in his quest to reactivate some stagnant accounts were starting to pay off. He'd received a number of small orders, which he made sure were expedited. For some reason, everything had been working out on all fronts, except his love life, but he could accept that, at least for now. He felt truly content.

The evening before they were to leave on the cruise, Gary was about to get in bed when his phone rang. "Hey, aren't you in bed yet?" Who else but Phillip? His new friend had really wormed his way into his life.

"I was just about to try to sleep, but I don't know how well it's going to work. What about you?" He'd thought about asking Phillip to come over for a little friendly fun, but that probably wasn't a very good idea. Since their encounter in Phillip's bedroom, they'd become really good friends, and that was more important that the quick relief of sexual tension. He really didn't need to complicate the relationship with what would inevitably turn into fun—but relatively meaningless—sex.

"I was wondering if you heard about my designs." He heard suppressed excitement in Phillip's voice.

"Not yet, but my supervisor was impressed, and he carries some weight. It may take some time, but they'd be fools not to buy them." Phillip's designs were brilliant. Gary was sure of it. "We might hear when we get back. Jack said he'd leave me a message and send an e-mail when he heard. Maybe I can get a signal on one of the islands. If I can, I'll check."

"I know you will."

Over time, Gary had found that Phillip's designs were like his babies. "And if they don't, we'll take them to another furniture manufacturer. I know people at a lot of them." Where all this confidence had come from, he wasn't sure, but he thought that Phillip had something to do with it. "I also think you should stop by some of the higher-end trendy shops and get their take on your designs. If they're interested that would help bolster your case in getting someone to look at the designs as well as in any negotiations to buy the designs."

"Damn, you're good."

"Actually I was wondering if you ever thought about producing your designs yourself."

"I looked into it, but I don't have the resources. I could probably get them produced overseas, but I always envisioned them as handmade pieces, rather than mass produced by the thousands and on sale at Walmart."

"Good point."

Phillip seemed to switch gears. "Do you have a ride to the airport?"

"Yeah, Tom and Bill are picking us both up in the morning."

"They are?" Phillip sounded confused.

"Tom called me today, and he said he talked to you a while ago and that he'd be willing to drive to save trips and parking fees at the airport."

"Now that you mention it, I do remember that now. I'm glad I called, or I'd have driven myself." Gary heard Phillip yawn and figured it was time to hang up.

"I'll meet you in front of my place at five." Gary hung up and climbed between the sheets, doubting he'd be able to get any sleep at all. But it turned out not to be a problem, and the next thing he heard was his alarm blaring in his ear a little after four. Cleaning up and showering, he checked that everything was packed and that he had a change of clothes and all the cruise documentation in his carry-on. One of the quirky things that Sean had warned them about was to make sure that they had their clothes for dinner the first night as well as a bathing suit in their carry-ons because their luggage might not be delivered to their cabin until sometime in the evening.

Making another pass through the apartment, he pulled his suitcase behind him and locked the door before heading to the elevator.

He saw Phillip waiting for him in the lobby, and a few minutes later, Tom and Bill pulled up. After loading everything in the back of their SUV, they were on their way. They'd managed to book a direct flight to San Juan, so after going through all the usual wait time and hassle at the airport, they boarded the plane, landing four hours later in San Juan. Claiming their luggage, they stepped from the terminal and into beautiful, glorious, warm weather, and sunshine.

They waited in line and grouped themselves into two taxis that whisked them through the city and along the waterfront. They passed gleaming high-rise hotels as they rode down palm-lined boulevards with tropical flowers blooming everywhere. Gary looked from one side of the car to another, taking in all the sights.

At the waterfront, the cab turned down an access road, and Gary found himself craning his neck upward as they passed a massive cruise ship with the Princess logo. As they went by, a gleaming white ship loomed overhead, and he looked farther up, realizing that the massive behemoth was to be his home for the next week. "Jesus, how will we ever find our way around that thing?" Tom and Bill both laughed, but Gary looked at Phillip and could almost see him thinking the same thing.

The cab pulled to the curb, and they paid the driver before getting out and retrieving their luggage to get into the boarding line, which wound halfway down the length of the ship.

As they approached the front, their luggage was taken and checked for the proper stateroom designation, and they passed into the terminal building. Their tickets were checked, passports verified, and sea passes issued. The agent explained that the sea pass acted as an onboard credit card and the key to their stateroom as well as their identification to get on and off the ship. Then they proceeded to the boarding ramp where their pictures were taken.

Phillip and Gary waited for the rest of the group as they wound their way up the long boarding ramp and onto the deck of the ship. They waited as a group for the security check and entry to the ship.

Gary used the perch to snap a few pictures of the scenery. As his camera panned back over the boarding ramp, a person coming up caught his eye. Gary lowered the camera and nudged Phillip, whispering, "Do you see the man coming up the ramp with the trampy-looking woman in a tank top?"

"Yea, what about him?"

"I swear that's the man I saw Mark letting into the store a few weeks ago." Both he and Phillip looked ahead to Mark and Tyler, but neither of them was looking in that direction, and the man and woman melded into the long line behind them.

The line began to move, and Gary found himself craning to see if he could see them farther back in line. The line ahead of them continued to move, and Gary gave up as they approached the ship. Their sea passes were scanned, carry-on bags X-rayed, and after walking through metal detectors, they were on the ship.

Sean and Sam gathered everyone together. "I suggest you go to your cabins, drop your bags, and then we can meet in The Catamaran for lunch. It's on the eleventh deck in the back of the ship." They started up the stairs, chattering excitedly back and forth until the roommates reached their deck.

Gary and Phillip wound down a long hallway along the side of the ship, looking for their cabin. They found it in the middle of the hall. Inserting his pass in the lock, Gary opened the door to a small, but extremely efficient cabin. Against the wall were two twin beds with small nightstands next to each one. A television was within easy view in a built-in, corner cabinet with shelves and drawers above and below. Farther back was a desk with more drawers and a banquette under a window overlooking the promenade, an indoor atrium down the center of the ship. A closet across from the bathroom, near the door, completed the cabin. Gary realized they could be very comfortable in this model of efficiency. They each selected a bed and set their carry-on bags on them before leaving the room and heading back toward the stairs.

The elevators were jammed, so they took the wide stairways up to the eleventh deck, easily finding the buffet. It was already crowded. Luckily, Sean and Sam were already seated at a table. Taking seats as well, Gary and Phillip looked around and talked while they waited for the others. It didn't take long for Mark, Tyler, Tom, and Bill to find the table, and they all got in line while Tom and Bill stayed behind to hold the table.

The buffet was huge, with food of every description and nationality. Gary quickly filled a plate and returned to the table so Tom and Bill could eat as well. It didn't take long for the rest of the party to return. Soon the table was full, and they were all talking excitedly about the trip ahead and what they were going to do that afternoon.

"After lunch Bill and I plan to put on our suits and make the most of the pool deck." Tom leered openly at his partner. Those two were still so much in love. "What about you guys?"

Bill began eating ravenously as Tom continued, "Then I thought we'd get in a workout. I'll need it after this lunch."

"I'd like to get some sun. How about you, Ty?" Mark moved close to Tyler, and Gary smiled, hoping whatever had been bothering them was over. They certainly looked happy.

"Sounds good to me," Gary replied. He didn't elaborate on the workout part of the plan, though. He hadn't spent any time in a gym since high school.

Echoes of agreement wound their way around the table as they all ate and chatted, commenting on the ship and the food. As he watched the people milling around, he spotted the man he'd seen earlier getting on the ship. Getting a better look at him, he was sure it was the same person. Looking over at Mark, Gary immediately saw the surprise on his face when he, too, recognized the man. He watched as they exchanged looks, and then the man ducked back to the far side of the buffet in what appeared to be quite a hurry. Gary continued to watch Mark as his expression went through a number of emotions, but the one he expected to see wasn't there. He'd have expected fear or embarrassment if Mark was having an affair, but neither was present. Mark was almost smiling. Maybe Phillip was right, and it wasn't what he'd thought. He was still curious as to what was going on, but he felt himself relax for Tyler and went back to his lunch.

Gary restrained himself from going for seconds—he'd have to be seen in a bathing suit after all—and continued talking until they were ready to leave. It wasn't long before Gary found himself in his swim trunks standing on the main pool deck, surrounded by throngs of people in their bathing suits. Suddenly he wanted to do nothing but hide. His legs and arms were skinny, his skin white as a sheet, and the deck was filled with tanned, toned men and women. At least that was how it appeared to Gary.

"It's fine. You're fine, Gary."

He looked down at himself and then over at Phillip, who looked like sex personified in a small square-cut bathing suit that left almost nothing to the imagination. "That's easy for you to say."

Phillip leaned close to Gary's ear. "If I hadn't found you attractive, I wouldn't have taken you to bed." Phillip's voice was the same tone he'd used in bed. This time, while nice, it had little effect, and Gary definitely knew he'd made the right choice. "So let's find us a couple of deck chairs, and I'll rub lotion on your back so you can start working on a tan."

Skeptical, Gary followed Phillip through the people to a set of empty chairs, and they spread out to save some for their friends. As soon as they were situated, Phillip began rubbing lotion on his back, and Gary returned the favor, lying on the lounge, listening to the splashes and laughter coming from the pool.

A set of thick legs entered his vision and he looked up, spying Bill standing next to his lounger. Gary watched as Bill pulled off his shirt, and had to stop his gasp. The man was incredible, strong, and toned, putting most of the men around the pool to shame. *I hope I look that good when I'm nearly fifty.*

Mark and Tyler joined them a few minutes later, nearly joined at the hip, both of them smiling like newlyweds. Gary rolled over and sat so he could look out over all the people gathering around the deck. People were running around, bounding between the two swimming pools and the numerous hot tubs.

"Looks like you have an admirer," Phillip whispered from the next lounge, as he motioned with his head toward the bar. "Just sweep your eyes."

Gary did as Phillip directed, seeing a tall man with a large tattoo on his broad shoulder peeking back at him. His hands were behind his back, and he appeared to be half-looking at the ground. Gary peeked at the man, but his attention didn't turn away immediately. Gary looked to one side and then swept his eyes back to the stranger, and to his surprise, he still appeared to be looking at him.

Gary looked at Phillip, certain the man was looking at one of the other people in their group. He certainly couldn't be looking at him.

"Someone's interested," Phillip teased as he resettled in the sun.

"He's probably looking at you." There was just no way that anyone would look at him that way, not with all the gorgeous men around.

Phillip's head turned slightly to peek. "Nope, he's definitely looking at you. He's being really shy about it, but he's definitely looking,"

Every time Gary would look, he'd turn away and scan over the crowd, but out of the corner of his eye, he could see the handsome man looking back over at him. His head stayed down and it looked like he was almost trying to melt into the background. They played that game for a while until someone tapped the man on his tattooed shoulder and said something to him. Slowly he followed his companion and drifted out of sight.

Chapter 5

"COME on." A light swat on his butt made him jump. "It's gym time."

"Maybe for you." Gary returned to the happy thoughts of the man he'd seen earlier—that is, until an ice cube made its way under his bathing suit. Gary couldn't remember moving that fast in a long time, jumping and squirming as he retrieved the coldness from his butt crack. "Hey!" Gary glared at a grinning Phillip.

"It'll be fun. Besides, after that lunch and with the huge dinner you're going to eat later, we'll need it." Phillip patted his flat stomach. "Don't want to lose our girlish figures, now do we?"

"Smart ass," Gary said, swatting at Phillip and missing. "I don't have workout clothes." He figured that would be the end of that.

"We've got an extra T-shirt and shorts," Tom piped in, and Gary had to stop himself from scowling at his friend.

"Fine." Gary knew a losing argument when he was in one. Getting up, he grabbed his towel and followed Tom and Bill to their cabin.

Phillip was already changed when he returned to their cabin. Gary ducked into the bathroom and changed before following Phillip to the gym and spa area. Entering, he found himself standing in the middle of the small, posh gym, and wondered what the hell he was supposed to do.

Tom must have seen his lost look because he walked right over. "Bill and Phillip are going to lift. I thought you could do a light circuit with me." Gary nodded, and Tom explained what they were going to do and how to use the machines. "We'll go through the routine four times and then quit. Use light weights to get your muscles used to the movement. It will also keep you from getting sore."

He sat himself on the row machine. After setting the weight like Tom had told him, he pulled the handles toward him, doing the ten reps Tom suggested. "You're doing great. Now move to the leg extension," Tom said from the next machine.

Gary sat at the machine and looked around the gym, scanning the scenery. He lifted his legs and began his set as a handsome man walked in front of him. Gary followed him with his eyes, realizing he was the man who'd spoken to the tattooed man on the deck. He continued the set and watched the man as he was joined by a walking god in a string tank and shorts. Finishing his set, Gary craned his head to see if the other man was nearby, and sure enough, he walked into the gym, joining the two other men.

Gary spoke to Phillip as he walked by. "God, this ship has great scenery."

"Tell me about it." Phillip came closer. "See the guy in the string tank? He's been on the cover of every fitness magazine in the country." Gary watched as Phillip practically drooled on himself. "Breathtakingly sexy doesn't begin to describe the man." Phillip's head panned around the room. "I see your admirer's here," Phillip teased as he went back to his workout.

Gary moved to the lat pulldown machine, but he found himself watching the three men, trying not to be obvious. Two of the men appeared to be a couple, their glances and small touches giving them away, but the tattooed man....

"Would it be all right if I worked in with you?" There he was, standing right next to him, his voice warm and very tentative, almost cautious.

"Sure." Gary finished his set and got up, trying to disguise his excitement. He actually peeked down to make sure he wasn't going to embarrass himself.

The man sat at the machine, adjusted the weight, and began his movement, and what movement it was. Gary found himself watching as those powerful back muscles stretched and contracted beneath the thin shirt. Good God, he could feel his blood flowing south. He forced himself to look away and move on to the chest exercise.

"Some view, huh?" Phillip's breath tickled his ear.

Gary just nodded. Everyone he looked at, even his friends, were all freaking incredible. Gary thought he should just give up and find some place to read until they were done.

"Don't even think about it," Phillip admonished as though he could read his mind.

With a huff, Gary began the chest exercise and finished his set.

"You should put your arms up a little."

Gary lifted his eyes and saw the tattooed man standing by him again. "You'll feel it through here more if you do." He demonstrated, running his hand across his ample chest, but his eyes remained glued to the floor and his hands slipped behind him when he wasn't talking. "Would you like me to show you?"

"Please." Gary got up, and he sat down, adjusting the weight and lifting his elbows before squeezing his arms along with his chest. Gary thought his eyes would bug at those bulging muscles and that shoulder tattoo rippled with strain.

"You try it." He got up slowly and stepped back, allowing Gary to use the machine. Gary sat and tried to replicate his position. "Lift your arms just a little more."

Gary felt the man's hands on his elbows, applying a small amount of pressure, but Gary felt the touch like an electric charge, zinging right through him. Squeezing his muscles he performed the movement, going through another rep.

"Do you feel it here?" A finger glanced over his upper chest. Gary nodded, his mouth suddenly going dry.

"Th-thank you." Gary got up and smiled at the man, not sure what else to say. Forcing his eyes away, he moved on to his last exercise in the circuit.

He spent the next half-hour going through the program Tom had devised, acutely aware of the tattooed man wherever he went. It was almost like his body was a compass needle and his tattoo had been applied with magnetic ink.

After working out, Gary and his friends relaxed in the steam room and sauna before changing back into their bathing suits and heading to the solarium for swimming and soaking in the kid-free hot tubs.

"Tomorrow we spend at sea," Sean began. "There'll be all kinds of activities and games."

"I saw a dodge-ball tournament on the sports deck for tomorrow afternoon. Is anybody interested?" Phillip piped in, already a bundle of energy. "Gary, are you game?"

The last thing Gary wanted to do was play a game that reminded him of middle school, but all the other guys agreed to play, so Gary went along. "I'll play, but I'm not very good." *More like scared to death of the ball.*

"Great, I'll enter us as a team." Phillip smiled and grabbed Gary around the waist, pulling him back into the water.

"There's also a climbing wall, mini golf, rollerblading, and a ton of other stuff."

Gary looked at Sean. "How do you know all this?"

"There's a schedule for today and tomorrow in your cabin along with a ship's map."

The undulating water felt good to Gary as he paddled around. Dunking his head, he surfaced and tasted salt water on his lips. No wonder the water felt so soft.

They swam for a while, and Gary thought to himself how wonderful it felt to have a group of friends who accepted him, and how nice it was to be part of that group. After their swim, they all returned to their cabins to change. The guys were hungry after their workout, so they hit the buffet for a small snack and then wandered the ship, exploring the decks before meandering their way to the dining room for the late-dinner seating.

In the lavish dining room, they found their assigned table and sat down. Their waiters introduced themselves, passed out the evening's menus, and took drink orders. The entire group talked and laughed, and from the sounds around them, others were having an equally good time.

"Hey, Gary, don't look now, but your admirer is at the next table." Gary turned slightly, and sure enough, the three men he'd seen in the gym were seated next to them. As he watched, another man and a woman joined them. The man must have seen Gary looking because he came right over to their table. "Hi, guys. I'm Lonnie and this is my fiancée Cory." He shook hands with everyone at their table and didn't blink when the couples introduced themselves.

Indicating his table, Lonnie made introductions. "Hey, ya homos, get over here." Gary was shocked, but the three men walked over, smiling. "This is Dan—"

Dan smacked Lonnie on the shoulder. "Don't pay any attention to Lonnie. The man was born without the gene that censors speech. This is my partner Gene and our friend Scott Haworth." Everyone shook hands, but Gary felt Scott hold his hand a little longer than was necessary, and Gary found that he didn't want to let it go. At least he knew his name and didn't have to refer to him in his mind as "the tattooed man" any more.

After talking briefly, they returned to their table as the waiters brought drinks and began taking orders for dinner. The menu choices were tantalizing, and Gary found himself unable to choose from all the great-sounding dishes. "You can get more than one," Sean said with a smile, and Gary looked to their waiter who explained that they could have whatever they wanted.

"You're kidding." Gary could barely believe it.

"Please, get whatever you like." They all ordered, and the waiters brought their first courses.

An appetizer and two entrees later, Gary was stuffed and extremely happy. Almost everyone declined dessert, and they left the table. Gary found himself looking to see if Scott was still eating, but the next table was already empty.

"I'm going to try my luck in the casino. Would you be my good luck charm?" Tom put an arm around Bill's waist as they left the dining room. Gary hadn't been in a casino before, so he followed Tom and Bill as they walked up to a craps table, and Tom bought some chips. Lonnie was playing as well, and Gary looked around. Sure enough, he spotted Scott standing back from the table, his back to the wall.

"Hi, Scott." Gary walked around the table, standing next to him. "Don't you play?"

He shook his head. "Don't really know how."

Gary smiled up at the tall, broad man. "Me neither." His heart practically skipped a beat when he got a smile in return. "Is this your first cruise?"

"Yeah. Never done anything like this before." A machine near them began ringing and Scott jumped slightly.

"You okay?"

"Yeah." This time he nodded as he answered. "I'm just not used to being around people like this."

Gary was about to ask if Scott wanted to take a walk with him on deck, but Gene and Dan joined them and told Scott they were heading up to their cabin. Scott smiled at Gary and said good night. Gary found himself following the movement of Scott's incredible backside until he disappeared from view... again.

"You let him get away." Phillip nudged his hip as he joined them. A cheer went up from the table. It appeared that both Tom and Lonnie were doing well, because the dice were rolled again, followed by another cheer.

"Didn't have much choice."

"He sure watches you."

"Don't know why." For the life of him, Gary couldn't figure out what a hunk like Scott could find interesting in him, but he sure seemed to. "But if he's interested, I'm not going to run away."

"That's the spirit." Phillip slapped him on the back happily as another cheer went up from the table.

Gary rejoined his friends, watching as the run at the craps table continued. Eventually, of course, it came to an end, but apparently not before Tom had won a significant amount of money. Gary watched as he picked up his chips, tipping the croupier.

"I think that's enough for one night." Tom was all smiles, an arm around Bill's waist, keeping his good luck close. "We'll see you in the morning."

Gary said his good-nights as well, as Phillip excused himself to head to one of the clubs. He'd invited Gary to go with him, but he had passed. Stepping out of the smoky casino, he wasn't in the mood for bed, so he headed up, deciding on a walk on deck.

Warm breezes blew across the slowly rocking ship, the effect almost as soothing as a lullaby. There were still a few people swimming and in the whirlpools on the otherwise deserted pool deck.

Slowly walking around he passed couples and a few kids who ran past him. Mostly, things were quiet. The runners who had claimed this part of the deck earlier in the day were gone. Walking along the port side, toward the bow of the ship, he passed beneath the bridge and saw a lone figure standing at the rail. Gary knew almost instinctively that it was Scott. The slightly bent posture and the way his head tilted down were clues, but also the hair that draped almost to his shoulders in luxurious waves. Half the women Gary knew would give their eyeteeth for the man's hair.

"Not tired?" Gary asked just above a whisper. Still, Scott jumped, whirling around to him, eyes wide as a deer in headlights.

"Sorry, no." He calmed and turned back to look as the lights of San Juan faded into the distance. "Not ready to sleep yet."

"It's a beautiful night. The moon and stars seem so close, almost like you can reach out and touch them."

Scott sighed softly, but didn't say anything. Thinking he wanted to be alone, Gary backed away.

"I guess I'm not much company," Scott said. "I just don't know what to say most of the time."

Gary laughed softly. "And some people say way too much."

He heard a soft chuckle from Scott, deep and rumbly in his chest. "Whatever Lonnie thinks just comes out in a steady stream. At least he's entertaining, and half the stuff his says is for effect anyway." Scott turned, and Gary got a good look at his handsome face. He had full lips and deep, dark eyes. "He has friends who have a two-year-old daughter, and they made the mistake of asking Lonnie and Cory to baby-sit. When they picked her up, she was asleep. The next evening they took Lonnie to dinner as a thank-you. When they walked in the restaurant, their Megan runs up to Lonnie, jumps into his arms, and in her little girl voice says, 'Wonnie, dingleberry, bing bing.' Complete with an obscene hand gesture. The parents were speechless, but Lonnie just laughed his fool head off and continued encouraging her throughout dinner."

Gary started to laugh. He just couldn't help himself. "You're kidding, right?"

Scott raised his hand. "Honest to God. I wouldn't believe it myself, but I was there."

Gary clutched his side, he was laughing so hard, but he managed to choke out, "The poor parents." Gary kept laughing. The image of the little girl just wouldn't leave his head.

Scott turned back toward the rail, his laughter fading away. Somehow Gary suspected he'd just gotten a small glimpse into Scott's personality that few people ever saw. The man had actually told a story, and Gary figured it was his turn, but he didn't really have any good stories to tell, so he told Scott about some of his clients and Mrs. Hueners.

"She emigrated from Hungary after the war and lives in my building. Her husband died a few years ago. She can never remember anyone's name, so she calls everyone Sweetie-Katchka. At first I was honored, until I realized she did it with everyone, including the mailman and the guy who cleans the halls. Whenever I see her, she remarks how thin I am, and once a week she brings me food to try to fatten me up." Gary saw Scott smile, and he continued. "She sounds like one of the Gabor sisters, and at the last tenants' meeting, I actually heard her go up to a man and compliment him on his mustache, or so she thought, telling him in her rich Hungarian accent, that he had a nice pussy-tickler."

Gary lost it, and to his relief, Scott did as well, both of them doubling over, holding their sides in complete belly laughter. It took a while, but they both recovered and fell silent. At one point a man walked by, and Scott pointed. The man had a mustache, and they both began laughing again. Eventually the laughter died away, replaced by the sounds of the ship and sea.

They seemed to have run out of things to say, and they both turned back to look out over the now moon-dappled water. Scott's hand rested on the rail, and Gary put his own on top of it, looking at the big man's face. He thought he saw a smile curl around the edge of Scott's lips as they stood there quietly together, watching the waves glimmer in the moonlight.

Chapter 6

GARY woke to the sound of a buzz saw in the next bed. Peeking at his nightstand, the clock read two-fourteen. "Phillip." He reached across and shook him by the shoulder.

"What?" His roommate sounded like a small child.

"You're snoring so loud the neighbors are complaining." Gary resettled in his bed, hoping he could get some sleep.

Phillip went into the bathroom, returned with a white strip on his nose, and climbed back into bed. "Sorry."

The soft rocking of the ship lulled Gary to sleep and the next thing he knew a shrill ringing in his ear pulled him out of a wonderful dream that involved Scott, one of the hot tubs, and absolutely no clothing. He heard Phillip moving and the ringing stopped.

"Yeah." Gary burrowed back under the covers as Phillip talked on the phone. "Okay, I'll tell him." Gary heard Phillip hang up the phone and then get out of bed. "Everyone's meeting in half an hour for breakfast."

Gary looked at the clock again and groaned. He was still tired, but managed to get himself moving anyway. At least he'd slept. Phillip disappeared into the bathroom, and Gary began getting dressed as Phillip's voice traveled through the door. "Tom said that he already ran into Lonnie and they were going to join us as well."

That lit a fire under Gary, and he suddenly began sorting through his clothes, wanting to look his best. The bathroom door opened, and Phillip stepped out. "Stop tearing everything apart.

Scott likes you, and I don't think it's because of your wardrobe. Just be yourself."

Gary knew he was right, and found a plain T-shirt and comfortable pair of shorts. Moving into the bathroom, he cleaned up and dressed. Phillip was waiting for him when he emerged, and together they headed to the buffet.

The rest of their group was already there along with Scott. Lonnie and team were there as well, but Gary stopped looking after he saw Scott. Joining the buffet line, he got his food and returned. To his pleasure, the chair next to Scott was empty, and he sat down, smiling a good-morning.

Multiple conversations swirled around the table, with Lonnie launching into another of his stories.

"Do you have plans for this morning?" Scott asked quietly, but for Gary he might as well have been shouting.

Gary swallowed his eggs. "No."

"I was wondering if you'd like to try the climbing wall... you know... with me?" Gary couldn't get over how shy and unassuming Scott was.

"Yes. I need to warn you, though; I've never done anything like that before." Gary had seen people climbing the day before, so he knew they used harnesses and stuff. He just hoped he didn't make himself look foolish.

"It's really fun, and there are paths set up for various experience levels." Scott's eyes were shining with excitement, and Gary put his hand on Scott's like he'd done the night before. "You'll really do it?"

"As long as I get to watch you first." Gary was so enthralled with Scott, he hadn't noticed that everyone else at the table had stopped talking and was looking at them. Gary looked around the table, and the conversation started again. Scott was obviously shy and didn't need to be stared at.

Gary had finished his breakfast and was getting up from the table when he spied Mark's mystery man again. Mark smiled and gave him a small wave, and this time Tyler saw and glared first at the man and then at Mark. Tyler threw his napkin on the table and began following the man. Mark got up and intercepted Tyler as he approached the exit to the dining room. Gary was too far away to hear what was being said, but Tyler's posture was rigid. Finally, Gary saw Mark lead Tyler away, and he hoped they were going to be able to clear the air.

"What was that about?" Sean asked as he got up from his seat.

Everyone shook their heads except Phillip, who remained remarkably quiet and suddenly seemed very interested in his empty plate. Sam noticed right away. "Do you know something?"

To Phillip's credit, he got up. "It's not for me to say."

The conversation wound its way back to semi-normal as they exited, people making plans. Gary found that Scott stayed with him, and when they left the dining room, Gary saw Mark and Tyler standing in the empty game room. Tyler's stance was visibly more relaxed, and as Gary watched, Tyler pulled Mark into a hug. They saw the other couple and motioned for them to come inside. "Is everything okay?" Gary asked from the door.

Tyler smiled broadly, holding Mark next to him. "Everything's fine."

"Are you going to go rock climbing?"

Tyler looked at Mark, his smile brightening further. "I think we're going to pass. We've got something more important to do." From the looks on both their faces, Gary had a pretty good idea what that was, so he and Scott excused themselves and made their way to the stern.

There was a line for the rock climbing, so they filled out the forms and got their gear on, waiting their turn. Scott did indeed go first, and Gary watched as he got into position and began climbing. For a big man, he was quite agile, and he made it to the top with relative ease, ringing the bell before being lowered to the ground.

Then it was Gary's turn. He walked to the man holding the safety rope, who snapped it on to Gary's harness and asked, "Have you done this before?" Gary told him he hadn't. "Then use the large green path."

Gary walked to the wall and began to climb. Using his hands and feet, he lifted himself up one green chunky thing at a time. After a while, he turned to look down and almost fell off the wall. He hadn't realized how high he was.

"Keep going; you're doing great." Gary realized it was Scott, and he looked upward, climbing closer and closer to the top. The bell was near his grasp, and Gary reached out and gripped the handle. The bell clanged, and he let go, descending back to the ground.

"Good job." The attendant unhooked the safety latch, and Gary walked to where his friends were waiting and collected pats on the back. Gary removed the safety harness and handed it to the desk attendant before watching Dan and Gene challenge each other to a race to the top. Gene won, but just barely.

"Did you like it?" Scott asked.

"It was really fun. I wouldn't have thought I'd like it, but I really did." They watched as Sam and Sean gave it a try, with Sam easily making it to the top, and Sean making it as well, but with a few struggles. "What's next?" Gary asked with a smile. This day was turning out to be more fun that he'd expected.

Gary spent the rest of the morning on a lounge chair on the main pool deck, with Scott on the lounger next to him. Gary looked over at him every few minutes, taking in the smooth, tanned skin and the muscles. He really wanted to know what it would feel like to run his hands over them, to have that tattooed arm sliding around his waist. The man was definitely handsome. Gary thought the term "sex on wheels" applied as well. Once again, Gary let his eyes wander. A light sheen of oil and sweat made Scott's skin glisten in the sun.

Scott didn't say a lot, but his face was expressive, and he'd made an effort to stay near Gary all morning. The attention was nice and spoke volumes, even if Scott didn't.

"I was thinking of going for a soak." Gary sat up and took a gulp of water, watching as Scott stood up. His long, thick legs, covered in a dusting of black hair, his narrow waist, broad shoulders, and those waves of black hair made Gary's mouth go dry again, and he took another gulp of water as he averted his eyes and tried to concentrate on something less sexy. The last thing he needed was to pop wood in his bathing suit.

Getting up himself, Gary followed that incredible backside. Damn, what he wouldn't give to see that butt without its cover of fabric.

People made room, and Scott slid into the bubbly water. Gary sat down next to him and relaxed. The sun, warm breezes, and hot bubbling water all worked to pull the last remaining tension from his body. He was glad he'd decided to come, and when he felt Scott's hand slide into his, he was even happier.

When someone slipped into the hot tub beside him, Gary turned his head and saw Tyler sitting next to him. "Is everything okay?"

Tyler grinned. "Everything's fine, except that I feel like a fool." Tyler scooted over and Mark joined them, settling next to Tyler, both men appearing extremely happy.

Gary resettled and felt an arm slide behind him. Scott nudged him close, and Gary found himself leaning against the big man. It had been a long time since he'd had someone to be close with, and Gary found himself wanting to get to know Scott better... much better. He wasn't sure the shy man was ready for that, but the hand-holding and the arm around his waist gave him hope. Gary figured he'd let Scott set the pace. He just hoped it wasn't too slow. They only had a week, after all.

After sunbathing and bubbling for a while more, the group met for lunch at the buffet. Phillip reminded everyone that the dodge-ball tournament was at one. When they'd eaten, Scott excused himself. Gary had been hoping Scott would watch, but he sensed the man needed some time alone.

Gary went with the rest of the guys to the sports deck. There were already three other teams signed up. Gary's team won the first game, but at a cost. Tyler got hit with a ball and ended up with a bloody nose.

"See if Scott will play." Phillip pointed to the far side of the court.

Gary smiled—Scott had come after all. "I'll ask." Gary walked around to where Scott was standing as the other two teams played their game. "Would you join our team?"

"I don't want to intrude on your friends." There was that shyness again.

"They asked if you'd like to play." Gary held out his hand, and Scott nodded, walking back with Gary and signing the team roster as the other game ended. The same team they'd defeated lost, so they were out.

The referee took the court. "The finals are a best-of-three playoff. We'll start in a few minutes." The teams filed onto the court. With a whistle, the game started. Red balls flew from one end of the court to the other. Gary actually managed to get an opponent out, but couldn't get out of the way of a shot himself. The rest of the game, he watched Scott. The powerful man moved like a cat, all grace and economy of movement. Thick legs corded when he stepped, and his shoulders and chest undulated when he threw.

They won the first game, but lost the second. In the last game, the other team ganged up on Scott and then picked off other team members one by one. It didn't look good. But the tide turned when Gary caught a flubbed throw, and Scott was able to get back in the game. It was now two against two, until Gary got hit in the hip. Scott managed to get one of the opponents, and then it was down to one on one. The team boundaries disappeared, and the two men chased each other around the court as both teams yelled encouragement. Scott dodged a throw and tossed off balance, hitting the other player on the foot. They'd won.

It was no *Chariots of Fire,* but they still celebrated. Gary found himself hugged by Scott, and the world stopped. Scott's body pressed against him, his scent filling Gary's nose, activating something deep inside him, and Gary became excited.

The referee's whistle called him back to reality, and Gary walked to the side of the court, hiding behind Scott until he could get his errant, but excited, body under control.

Each team got medals with the ship's logo. Gary held his gold-colored medal, smiling up at Scott. If nothing else, he had an interesting souvenir.

They left the court, and Gary pulled Scott aside and around to a deserted section of the rails. "Thank you for playing, it was fun." Scott's scent went right through him.

"You're welcome. I had fun too." Scott replied but looked confused as to why he'd been dragged here.

Gary suddenly felt really shy, but girded his nerves. "I wanted to ask you something. But I'm not sure how." Gary found himself looking around nervously. "Oh, hell." Gary stood on his tiptoes and kissed Scott softly. It was little more than a peck, but it seemed to have the desired effect. Scott smiled and leaned forward, returning Gary's kiss, and this one was definitely more than a peck.

Gary felt like he was being devoured, the energy and need behind the kiss nearly knocking him off his feet. His body zinged, and his mind soared as he felt Scott's lips tug on his before pulling away. Gary was about to go for a repeat when he heard someone approaching and backed away. The footsteps stopped, and Gary saw an expression of surprised confusion on Scott's face followed by something that looked like shame.

"What the fuck are you doing here?!!!"

Gary turned around to see who'd spoken and saw a small man with a look of disgust directed at Scott.

When Gary turned around again, Scott was gone, and Gary only saw his retreating backside as he hurried away. Without thinking, Gary followed, jogging to catch up. "Scott, who was that?"

Scott stopped and turned around, his face a mask of despair. "Stay away from me, Gary. I'm no good... for anyone." Then he was gone, hurrying through the doors.

Gary felt lost. He went back to see if he could find the man who started this, but couldn't find him. As he searched, he saw the guys sitting together enjoying a drink.

"We're celebrating our victory." Phillip grinned in a mock-macho voice. "That, and Mark was telling us about the drama." Phillip looked around. "Where's Scott?"

Gary shrugged and sat down, trying his best to disguise his confusion from his friends. He didn't want to be a downer.

"So, where was I?" Mark asked before going on. "Oh, yeah, I remember. About four months ago, I got a call from a potential client about a portrait. I met with him and didn't really think too much about it." Mark paused for a second. "I can't tell you anything more about him, but suffice it to say the contract requires that I keep the portrait and any information about him confidential."

Tyler interjected, "He's been working on it whenever they could get together, and I thought," he said, having the good sense to blush, "that Mark was having an affair."

Mark gave Tyler a kiss. "Anyway, I find out the portrait is to be a nude, and he's really nervous and shy about it, but it's what his wife wants."

"So he added the confidentiality clause?" Gary asked.

"Yeah, also he was only available evenings and wouldn't allow any photographs. On top of that, I could only work on it when Tyler wasn't around." Mark's voice trailed off. "I'm only saying anything at all because of what happened earlier. The portrait's completed and paid for."

Mark turned to Tyler. "I hated keeping secrets from you, and I won't do it again." They kissed, and a chorus of awwws rose from the table.

Sam waved, and Gary followed his line of sight and saw Gene and Dan walking over. They looked serious, like there was something wrong. "Gary, have you seen Scott?"

Gary told them what happened, leaving out the kissing part. That was just for him. He could still feel the ghost of Scott's touch on his lips. "He seemed pretty shaken up." Worse than Gary did right now, that was for sure.

Gene was already hurrying down the deck, and Dan said a brief thank-you and quickly followed, leaving Gary even more confused than ever. As he watched them go, a strange thought occurred to him. *We're only one day into the cruise, and we've had all this drama. What's next?* From the conversation he'd heard at Mark and Tyler's party, there were still some surprises in store.

A waiter walked by, and Phillip ordered Gary a drink. "You look like you could use one." That was an understatement if he'd ever heard one. "It sounds as though you've already had an interesting day." Phillip smiled over at him, and when he didn't return it, Phillip became serious. "It'll be okay. Whatever upset him wasn't your fault." The others at the table echoed Phillip's sentiments.

"Gary." The table got quiet as the waiter brought his drink, and then Tom continued, "I've been watching Scott, and I know he's been hurt. I can see it in his face. Be patient with him, but be careful. That man, whoever he was, obviously knows something about Scott that we don't. I'm not saying he's right, I'm just saying that I don't want you to get hurt, and if he decides to open up to you, take it as an act of trust."

Gary nodded and sipped his drink, wondering what Scott could possibly have done to earn such hatred. Of all the things he thought of, Gary knew that reality often had a knack for handing him the worst.

Chapter 7

GARY spent the afternoon concentrating on having the best time possible. He and Phillip swam and soaked, running the waiters crazy for sodas and drinks. At one point, a hot tub emptied, and all the guys piled in. There was one notable absence, and that was Scott. Dan and Gene had returned, but when Gary asked about Scott, Dan had shrugged. "I don't know. He wasn't in his cabin, and we haven't heard from him." The two men joined them in the hot tub, but Gary found himself looking around constantly, hoping Scott would make an appearance. He didn't. There was nothing Gary could do, and that was the frustrating part. He'd asked Dan if he knew what was wrong, but he'd evaded the question. Obviously, whatever it was, it was something very personal to Scott.

The strength of the afternoon sun had begun to fade when Gary climbed out of the pool and grabbed his towel and other pool things, heading back to his cabin. He figured he'd work out with the guys before dinner. Entering his cabin, he slipped off his bathing suit and slipped on his workout clothes, well, what he had that passed for workout clothes. Grabbing his sea pass, he opened the door and practically ran straight into Scott, who looked like he had been about to knock on the door. Gary stopped and looked up into a pair of sad, confused eyes.

"Can we talk, Gary?" Scott asked.

"Sure." Gary stepped back into the cabin, and Scott followed, sitting on the edge of his bed.

Scott began pacing in the small space along the wall. "I... I need to tell you about some things that have happened to me, and I need you to let me get all the way through. You might not want to see me any more after I'm done, and I'll understand."

"You don't owe me anything, and you don't have to tell me anything you aren't ready for." Gary sat still and watched Scott as he continued circling the small space, waiting for him to say what he wanted to say.

Scott stopped walking and sat on the other bed. "About ten years ago, I was accused of raping a seventeen-year-old girl. She was a friend of one of my neighbor's daughters. One of her other friends identified a man who matched my description as the assailant. The victim was blindfolded during the assault, but her friend apparently saw the rapist leaving the apartment."

Gary saw Scott begin to breathe heavily and tremble a little, but he stayed where he was, even though his instinct was to comfort. He waited for Scott to continue.

"The police apparently botched a number of things during the investigation and were looking at a kid the girls went to school with. Then, to my shock, the witness identified me as the rapist. To make matters worse, I was home alone at the time of the rape, sleeping one off. I couldn't remember where I'd been, so no one could vouch for me. The police pounced on me as easy prey and built a case, eventually arresting me. I knew I was innocent and had never touched the girl, but that didn't seem to matter. I was arrested at work a few days later. I was barely making enough money to make ends meet, let alone hire a lawyer, so I got a public defender. I was innocent, and I knew it, but I couldn't prove it and kept praying that the nightmare would end. But it only got worse."

Gary saw Scott's bottom lip tremble a little, and he reached out and took his hand. "At trial, what little evidence I could present was thrown out on some sort of technicality, and the police had free rein, but I still thought I'd be okay because I was innocent. When the trial was over, the jury came back with a 'guilty on all counts' verdict. I almost passed out and fell back into my chair. When the judge passed sentence, he gave me the harshest penalty he could: forty years."

A tear rolled down the big man's cheek. "It practically killed my parents, but they stood by me. I was placed in a maximum security facility and spent the next year trying to figure out what the hell had happened." Scott sniffed and wiped his face. "Three years later I heard about this thing called the Innocence Project, and I got to work. I studied law in the prison library and began putting together the paperwork for an appeal. I also sent the Innocence Project a letter with everything I knew about my case."

Gary didn't know what to say, and he found himself riveted by the story and sickened by what had happened to Scott.

"A year later, my appeal was denied, and I heard from the Innocence Project that they were going to look into my case. During that time, my mother, the only person who regularly came to see me, died of cancer." Scott put his hands over his eyes, and his shoulders bounced as he cried. "I couldn't go to her funeral and had to say good-bye to her at night when no one could see my weakness." He croaked through his tears, and Gary found his throat tightening, realizing the courage it took to tell him this. "After her death, I almost gave up, but then I got a letter from the Innocence Project saying that they were seriously reviewing my case. One of their lawyers came to see me, and I told him everything I knew. Before he left, he said he'd see what he could do. Months went by, and I heard nothing. Finally, my father visited me and told me that there was biological material on the victim's clothes that was never tested for DNA and never revealed to the defense. I couldn't hug him because he wasn't allowed in the same room with me, but he smiled, and I saw hope in his eyes for the first time. More months went by, during which I later learned that they petitioned for the evidence, but the prosecutor denied them access to it, and it took more months for them to get the court to force them to turn it over. Once the clothing was tested, it showed that the DNA wasn't mine. And what's more, it matched a man on the FBI Wanted list for rape."

Scott looked up, his face now calm, and Gary felt the butterflies in his stomach. "I was innocent, and they'd been able to prove it. One morning I was rousted out of my cell and marched past all the other inmates toward the prison offices. Doors opened ahead of me, and I was put in a room and told to get dressed. On a bench, I found the same clothes I'd worn the day I entered prison. After I put them on, I knocked, and they let me out of the room and walked me out of the prison. It was then I saw my father and was able to hug him for the first time in nearly ten years."

Scott's face became calm. "My dad took me home, and I tried to get back to some form of normal life, but nothing was like I remembered. My dad tried to help me all he could, but he died three months later from the same kind of cancer that took my mother. It was then, about nine months ago, that I met Lonnie and Cory. He's a great guy and helped me meet people and get used to doing normal things again, and she sort of mothered me into moving on." Scott looked up and appeared to be waiting for Gary to say something, but Gary had no idea what to say.

Gary found his voice. "Did anyone," he said, swallowing, "hurt you while you were in prison?"

"No, thank God. I've always been big. A few guys tried, but I handled the first guy, and no one bothered me after that." Scott shrugged. "But some of the things I saw still give me nightmares." Scott lifted his head and looked to Gary and waited. When Gary didn't move, Scott got up to leave.

The movement spurred Gary into action. "Where are you going?"

"I told you I'd understand if you didn't want me around." Scott walked to the door.

"Scott." He turned around. "Don't go." Gary walked to him and put his arms around his waist, hugging him tight. "I don't want you to go."

Thoughts of everything Scott had been through gave him the chills, but the man he was holding made him feel nothing but warmth. Gary waited and finally felt Scott's arms around his back, returning his hug.

"I can't imagine what you went through, but you didn't do anything wrong," Gary said, looking up into Scott's eyes. "You're the strongest person I've ever known if you could survive that."

Gary stepped back and took Scott by the hand, pulling him back toward the bed. "Who was that guy on deck?"

"Frank Garrett, he's the brother of the victim. I found out after I was released that the thought of my getting out terrorized her so much that she killed herself. Even though I was proved innocent, she still believed I was the one who raped her. The police told me that she was obsessed that I was going to try to get to her again, and she killed herself. Her brother blames me for all of it."

Gary felt his anger rising. "If he does that again, I'll report him." Then another thought occurred to Gary. "How did he know you were on board? Or was it a coincidence?"

Scott shrugged. "I don't know."

"Did they ever catch the real guy?" Gary moved closer to Scott, resting his head against his shoulder.

"No. They know who he is, but Frank Garrett, the guy on deck, still blames me anyway." Gary felt Scott lean back against him.

"He can blame you all he wants, but you did nothing wrong." Gary ran his hand along Scott's arm. "Scott, can I ask you something?" He nodded, and Gary saw Scott turn toward him. "Do you feel the same thing I do? Like there's something special between us?"

Scott's eyes drooped slightly. "Yeah, as soon as I saw you, I wanted to meet you, but I didn't know how. Then I saw you in the gym, and Dan convinced me to talk to you."

"I'm glad he did." Gary leaned forward, moving closer to Scott, and their lips met. The room tingled with electricity, and Gary felt Scott kiss him back. Gary moved closer, his arms encircling Scott's neck as Scott held him close. His tongue explored the hard, full lips, and when Scott parted them slightly Gary took it as an invitation, and his tongue began to explore further.

Without warning, the door to the cabin opened, and Phillip walked in. With a huff of disappointment, Gary pulled away, but still held on to Scott.

"Sorry. I came to see if you were going to work out with us before dinner, but…."

Scott moved away slowly and stood up, still holding Gary's hand. "I shouldn't stay."

"Why?"

Scott leaned close to Gary's ear. He looked at Phillip and then back at Gary. "I want you too much." He stepped back and walked to the door. "I'll see you in the gym?"

Gary nodded and watched as Scott opened the door and left, looking back just as the door closed.

"Your timing is just wonderful, you know that?" Gary couldn't help smiling as he thought of what Scott had said.

"I said I was sorry."

"I know. I was just teasing." He was, but he was also disappointed. "Get changed, and we'll go on down to work out." Gary sat on his bed and waited for Phillip to get changed, anxious to meet Scott in the gym.

Walking into the workout area, Gary saw Scott, who looked like he was waiting for him. As he and Phillip left to put their things in the locker area, Gary saw the Frank guy striding in. He wasn't dressed to work out and appeared to be looking for Scott.

Gary followed him, and as he turned the corner to the workout area, what he found made him smile: a wall of flesh in the form of Dan, Gene, and Lonnie, their arms crossed in front of their chests. The three men glared at the man as he tried to look around them.

"Leave him alone, you miserable excuse for a hobbit." When Frank didn't back down, Lonnie let loose with a barrage of obscenity that not only called into question the guy's parentage, but the history of his entire family and even described what he'd do to his mother in particular. When Frank still didn't get the message, Lonnie stepped forward and kicked his leg in the air, his foot coming within an inch of Frank's body. "Leave him alone, or I'll kick your ass across the ship." The demonstration seemed to have an effect, because Gary saw Frank pale, and after some bluster, he turned to leave.

"You know what he did?" Frank yelled as he walked toward Gary. "He's a fucking criminal!" Before Gary could respond, Frank hurried outside.

The guys returned to their workout, each giving a stunned Scott a pat on the shoulder. "What's that look for?" Gary asked, as he followed Scott to one of the machines.

"They stood up for me." The expression of complete disbelief was hard for Gary to get over. But what Scott had told him explained a lot.

"Of course they did; they're your friends. And from the looks of it, good friends to have." Gary let his eyes wander to where the three of them were taking turns bench pressing the heaviest dumbbells the ship had and doing it with ease. "Do you want to join them? I know you'd get a better workout working with them than doing these machines with me." Scott looked over at the guys. "Go on. Besides, I can watch all those muscles you've got at work." Gary saw Scott blush and look down toward the floor. "Have fun."

Gary watched as Scott smiled at him and then joined the "big boys," as Gary went through the routine he'd done the day before. When he was done, the guys were still going at it, so he got on a treadmill and walked, looking out across the bow of the ship to the sea.

"Are you having a good time?" Bill stepped on and started the treadmill next to him.

"You bet!" He found himself grinning. He could hardly believe his luck. He'd met a handsome guy and was having an incredible time with his group of friends. "I'm glad I came."

Bill looked around. "Tom's fiftieth birthday is Wednesday, and I've got a surprise party planned for him. Sean and I have been working on it for weeks. He hates his birthday, keeps saying he doesn't need a reminder of how old he's getting." So that was what the snippet of conversation he'd heard at the party was about.

"I wish you'd told me sooner. I could have gotten him something." Gary immediately made a note to look for something at their first port of call.

"It's not necessary." Bill would have said more, but Gary saw Tom approaching. He got on the treadmill on the other side of Bill and their conversation turned to their plans for the following day. Tom, Bill, and some of the guys were planning to take a snorkeling excursion on Barbados. "We'll sail to Turtle Bay for snorkeling, and hopefully we'll see some sea turtles. There'll be drinks and snacks on the boat, and afterward they'll drop us off at one of the beaches," Bill explained. "Mark and Tyler are going with us as well, and I think Sean and Sam are booked too."

"What about Phillip?" Gary asked as he craned his neck to see what Scott was doing.

"I think he's going to a beach for the day," Bill supplied as he revved up his treadmill and began to run.

Gary wondered what Scott would like to do, and saw him finish a set and smile over at him. Gary motioned to him, and he came over.

"Did you have plans already made for tomorrow?" Scott shook his head. "Tom and Bill are going snorkeling tomorrow, and I was wondering if you'd like to go, too, you know… with me." God, he felt like a high school kid asking a girl on his first date. He peeked over and noticed Tom and Bill both doing their best to listen while trying to appear to be paying attention to something else.

"I'd like that." The words were tentative, and Gary was coming to realize that Scott's words were less important than the excitement in his eyes and the smile on his face.

Gary turned to the guys. "Do we book it through the ship?"

"That's probably best." Tom sped up his machine and began to run alongside Bill. Gary pressed the stop button on his; he'd had enough.

"Are you done?" Gary asked expectantly, and Scott nodded. "Ready to sauna?" Another nod, and Gary felt a surge of excitement as they headed toward the locker room. The thought of Scott nearly naked, sitting in the sauna getting all wet and sweaty, had him popping wood instantly. When they got into the locker room, Scott stripped off his clothes, and Gary got a good look at his incredible, dimpled butt before it was hidden from view by a towel... and only a towel. Gary had to wait until Scott left before stripping off his own clothes. Thinking unsexy thoughts, he wrapped the towel around his waist and headed for the sauna.

Those unsexy thoughts flew out the window when he entered the small, hot room and saw Scott sitting back, his towel resting low across his hips. Tempting fate, Gary sat where he could watch. Each breath filled Scott's powerful chest, expanding it, and Gary had to adjust things to keep them from becoming too obvious. That intricate, sexy tattoo shimmered with sweat in the soft light. The man was certainly handsome. Then Gary shifted his gaze, looking down at his own chest. He didn't have a gut, but his chest was largely flat, his hips bony, and his arms small and straight. There were no muscular curves and no bulges of strength. As he looked back at Scott, he wondered what the man saw in him. He knew he was more than what he looked like, but he couldn't help wondering. He saw Scott smile over at him, and he returned it, pushing his doubt away. If this gorgeous man was interested in him, he'd stop questioning it. They were on a cruise for a week; after that, the real world would take over.

He wanted the man—so badly. His outer strength and inner vulnerability, combined with the fact that he seemed like such a kind person, really appealed to Gary. He knew he couldn't rush it, but whenever he looked across the sauna at Scott's glistening skin, rivulets of water sliding down his chest, he had to stop himself from sitting on Scott's lap and licking those drops back to their source.

Gary shifted on the bench. He was becoming painfully hard, and as the towel got more and more damp, it was becoming more and more obvious. Getting up, he left the sauna, got a fresh towel, and moved to the steam room, which was blessedly empty, and he could think without Scott's hunkiness to look at for a few minutes.

The door opened, and Gary saw Scott poke his head in. "Tom says we probably need to get moving if we're going to get a quick snack." Gary nodded and the door closed, only to open again. "Uh, I wanted to ask if you'd sit with me at dinner." The man was so cute and looked all flustered.

"Of course." Gary smiled and got up. "Sort of like a first date." The term seemed to make Scott blush, but he nodded his head before closing the door again. The smile stayed in place as Gary showered and dressed.

Gary wandered the ship, exploring the huge vessel before returning to his room to get dressed for dinner. Tonight was one of the two evenings they had to dress up for dinner, and he had a date. Phillip looked him over and pronounced him handsome, with the help of one of Phillip's shirts and one of Tom's ties. He and Scott had agreed to meet on the promenade, and when he arrived, Gary found Scott waiting, looking good enough to eat in a black tuxedo. The clothes accentuated Scott's broad shoulders.

"Do I look okay?" Scott seemed really uncomfortable in the clothes. He wasn't squirming or pulling at the collar, but Gary could tell he wasn't at home in them.

"You look...." Gary tried to find the right words, but only "Wow" came out. Gary's cock had been half-hard since the sauna, and now it perked back up. "I'd kiss you right here, but we'd probably scare the straight people," Gary said, doing his best Hollywood Squares impression of Paul Lynde and smiled when Scott began to laugh. "You got it?" Gary's smile turned into a grin.

"I got it, funny man," Scott said with a smirk as the doors to the dining room opened and they walked inside.

"After dinner I need to stop and book our snorkeling for tomorrow," Gary said as they made their way through the room.

Dinner was amazing. Scott spent much of it with his hand resting on Gary's leg, the simple touch feeling warm and good. After filling up on shrimp cocktails and lobster, he and Scott walked along the deck. Clouds obscured the stars, but the light breeze felt nice, and in the Moon Bar, overlooking the entire ship, Gary felt Scott take him into his arms. The ship swayed like they were on the world's biggest dance floor. Live music began to play behind them and couples began to dance. Scott moved them to the music.

Gary heard a woman gasp and expected a mean comment, but got a surprise instead.

"Look, Ziggy, remember when we were that young?"

"You still are, Carol, you still are."

Gary looked into Scott's eyes, willing him to kiss him, and when he did, it felt like they were on the top of the world. Scott held him for a long time, swaying him to the music as others danced. Gary felt them begin to move off the dance floor, but nothing outside of Scott's touch mattered. He just knew he was with Scott and would go where he led.

Scott stopped them, and Gary looked around. "Where are we?"

"My cabin."

Chapter 8

"WOULD you?" Scott opened the door, and Gary followed him inside. A single light burned beside the bed. Scott's kisses started out gentle and remarkably soft, but they built into a hurried frenzy very quickly. Gary found himself pulling at Scott's bow tie, then sliding his hands down his shirt, parting the fabric before sliding the shirt and jacket off his arms. Scott's skin felt warm against his lips as he kissed trails across the powerful, defined chest. A firm nipple slid under his tongue, and Gary sucked gently. A hiss and a moan greeted him, and he repeated the motion, added his swirling tongue to the mix. Scott thrust his chest forward, and Gary obliged, giving him more stimulation.

Gary's hands stayed busy. Scott's belt opened under his fingers, and the fastener on his pants popped open. Scott continued making the most wonderful sounds as his pants slid down his legs. Shoes quietly hit the carpet, and Gary threw himself at Scott, both of them toppling on the bed. Gary wasted no time capturing Scott's lips. His own jacket slipped from his body and his shirt buttons opened. Gary sighed as his chest pressed to Scott's, skin to skin. A big hand slid down his back and cupped his butt, pressing their groins together. Gary stood up, toeing off his shoes as he shed his shirt and pushed down his pants, throwing them on the chair, leaving only his underwear on before pouncing on Scott in a haze of desire.

He just couldn't get enough of Scott. His hands wandered all over the man's body, hot skin flowing beneath his touch as he kissed and licked Scott's lips. Something inside his lust-clouded brain pulled him back, telling him to ease up. Gary opened his eyes and looked into Scott's, seeing a look of amazed confusion. "Sorry, I got carried away."

Scott's entire expression broke into a smile. "Did I do that to you?"

Gary nodded and smiled before nibbling on Scott's neck. "Uh-huh." Gary kept licking and kissing, his touch gentling, and he forced his body to stop sliding up and down on Scott. He wanted this to last, and he was suddenly very uncertain. "When was the last time you were with someone?" Gary looked into Scott's eyes, seeing tears welling in them.

"The night before I was arrested." Scott turned his head away.

"You have nothing to be ashamed of." Gary placed his hand on Scott's chin. "We won't do anything you don't want to do. Being with you is enough." All his life he'd been the weak one. He hadn't played sports, and if it hadn't been for his best friend's protection in high school, he'd have been a bully's dream. And now, for the first time, he felt like someone else needed *his* protection and guidance, like he was the one who had to look out for someone else, and he found he liked it.

"Are you sure?"

"More than sure," Gary whispered, as he brought their lips together, and he smiled into the kiss when he felt Scott's hands on his back, lightly stroking his skin. Gary decided he'd let Scott set the pace, so he began stroking his side and shoulders with the same intensity. When Scott's hand slid into his underwear to cup his butt, Gary increased the intensity of his kisses, moaning softly and nodding as Scott began to lower the fabric. "Whatever you want, Scott."

"Then I want you." Scott's size became a distinct advantage when he rolled them on the bed, pinning Gary to the mattress. The kisses continued, and Gary ran his hands along Scott's broad, strong back, sliding them down to the base of his spine and then up to his shoulders. Slowly he pulled away to look into Scott's eyes as he slipped his hands beneath the waistband of his boxers, asking permission before going any further. Scott nodded slowly, and Gary pushed the fabric down and off.

Scott knelt over Gary's body, and he saw and felt Scott's gaze as it passed over every inch of him. When Phillip had done the same thing a month earlier, he'd been self-conscious, but the adoring look in Scott's eyes banished that feeling from his mind. Scott wanted him just as much as he wanted Scott. It was almost too much for him to hope for, but it was true. Gary looked his fill as well. Reaching for Scott, he traced the outline of his chest and let his fingers slide down the trim stomach before curling around his length and running his fingers lightly over the silky hardness. Scott arched his back and hissed softly, so Gary repeated the motion until Scott's eyes closed, and Gary heard his breathing start to hitch.

"Please, not yet." The words squeaked out through Scott's gritted teeth, and Gary stopped, pleased that he'd been able to make Scott that excited that quickly. Like Scott, he wanted this to last, wanted to hear Scott moan his name again and again before he came. It was important to Gary that this be very special for Scott.

"What would you like, Scott?"

The question was met with a blank look. "I don't know." Then Scott began to laugh softly. "It's been so long."

Gary wriggled out from under Scott and settled him on his back on the bed. "Then let me." Gary kissed Scott's lips, then moved to his chest, swirling his tongue around a nipple. When Scott began to wriggle, he smiled and kept going, kissing his way down Scott's stomach to the nest of black curls above his magnificent cock.

Scott's eyes were already closed, and Gary could see him trying to control himself by measuring his breathing. Gary opened his mouth and slowly slid his lips down Scott's length. The skin was hot and flavored with an intense version of Scott's individual spice. Immediately small moans reached his ears, and he began to suck, sliding his lips up and down the shaft. As Scott's moans increased, Gary increased his own efforts.

Scott's stomach muscles contracted, and Gary stopped, sliding his lips away. He kept up that treatment for a while. Every time he thought Scott was close, he'd stop. The groans became louder whenever he'd stop, and the moans got higher when he'd resume. "You said you wanted this to last."

"Ga-ry." The frustrated whimper made his heart rejoice and his resolve crumble. With a grin, he took Scott deep, sucking hard and long. This time the moans were intense, and Gary kept up the pressure. Scott's hips began to thrust up from the bed, and Gary rode with him until, with a soft cry, he felt Scott climax hard. His mouth filled with Scott's unique flavor as he swallowed all he had to give.

Scott collapsed back onto the bed, completely limp. Gary let Scott's cock slip from his lips and brought their mouths together, sharing Scott's own flavor with him. Gary's hips began thrusting, sliding his length against Scott's hip and it took only a few strokes before his own climax hit him. Crushing his lips to Scott's, he felt Scott hold him tight as his desire and passion gripped him, and he spilled himself between them. Then it was Gary's turn to collapse, and he felt Scott hold him until they both fell asleep.

The sun peeking around the balcony curtains woke Gary, and he began to squirm, not remembering where he was or why there was a weight against his body. Looking around, he began to remember the night before, and he realized that Scott was the one holding him like he was a security blanket.

"No! Stop!" Scott began to thrash and the arm holding him began to swing in the air. It wasn't aiming for him and appeared to be swinging at some imaginary person.

"It's okay, Scott. It's Gary." He began to rub Scott's side gently, trying to bring him slowly out of whatever dream he was having. The hand slapped down right next to Gary's head, making the bed bounce with its force. He started to get concerned. "Scott, wake up. It's just a dream." He knew it wasn't good to wake him too abruptly—he might think Gary was the person from his dream. "Scott." He kept his voice level and soothing. "Scott, it's okay. Wake up." He ran his hand across Scott's cheek, and Scott held it to his face, so Gary continued stroking the stubbly skin.

"Gary?" Scott's eyes opened, and he looked around like a startled animal. "What happened?" Scott sat upright. "I didn't hurt you, did I?"

Gary shook his head. "You were having a nightmare. Do you remember?"

"Unfortunately. It happens all the time." Scott settled back onto the bed. "There are things I saw when I was in prison, and when I sleep, I see them again."

"Does it happen every night?"

"Sometimes. After I got out, I saw a therapist, but he was no help at all. I saw what I saw, and I keep playing it over and over. Hearing them screaming and begging for them to stop." Scott closed his eyes, and as Gary watched he seemed to hold them shut with all his might, like if he didn't open them, he could will the images away. "There are things I did in prison, things I'm not proud of, but the things I keep playing over and over are the things other people did that I couldn't stop."

Gary could tell Scott's emotions were just below the surface and that he was having a tough time keeping them under control. He wasn't sure if he should encourage Scott to let them out or not. "If you want to tell someone about them, I'll listen. But you are responsible for you and what you did, and, more importantly, what you didn't do. You didn't hurt anyone who wasn't trying to hurt you first." Gary stopped and waited for some sort of acknowledgment from Scott, and then he continued. "And you didn't do anything to deserve being in prison in the first place." Gary slowly pressed Scott against the mattress. "That you hear those voices and feel the way you do means that you're a good person with a good conscience."

"It doesn't scare you?" Scott's eyes were huge pools of warm brown, shimmering with unshed emotion.

"Why should it? You'd never hurt me." Somehow Gary knew that Scott would hurt himself long before he'd ever intentionally hurt him, and with that realization, he knew he felt exactly the same. Circumstances and things they had no control over might cause pain, but he would never do it on purpose.

A rowdy knock on the door made Scott jump beneath him, and Gary reluctantly shifted off of him, his body missing the warmth and touch immediately.

"Scott, are you up yet?" Dan's voice called through the door. "We need to find Gary and get moving."

Gary pulled on his pants and walked to the door, opening it just a crack before peeking his head into the opening. "He's up." Gary couldn't keep the smile off his face, particularly at the surprised and pleased look on Dan's face.

"The tour leaves in less than an hour, and you'll need to get something to eat first."

Gary swore softly. In his distraction the evening before, he'd forgotten to book the trip. "Okay. Where are we meeting?" He could already hear Scott moving around behind him.

"We're on our way up to the buffet. We'll wait for you there."

"Okay." He shut the door and turned around to see a nearly dressed Scott pulling on his shirt. Gary began picking up his clothes from the various places they'd landed. "I feel so dumb. I forget to book the trip last night."

Scott didn't miss a beat. "Then we'll pay at the dock. They'll have room. Don't worry." Scott smiled disarmingly.

"I'll meet you in the dining room." He was still disappointed with himself, but stood near Scott and kissed him softly, thankful he'd been so understanding.

Gary finished pulling on his clothes, and after another quick kiss, hurried out the door and toward his cabin. As he approached, he saw Phillip closing the door. "I was just going to look for you." Gary rushed inside and began pulling off his clothes, hanging up his good clothes and pulling on a bathing suit while Phillip put Gary's bag on the bed. Gary hurried and threw in a change of clothes before pulling on a pair of shorts over his swimsuit. He grabbed a T-shirt before slipping into his shoes. "Thanks, Phillip."

"No problem." They finished their packing, and Gary grabbed his sea pass, ID, and money before leaving the cabin with Phillip. Shutting the door, they walked quickly to the elevators and managed to catch a car almost immediately to the eleventh deck.

They had little difficulty finding the guys, and Scott handed him his tour ticket with a smile. "How much do I owe you?" Gary asked quietly, pulling out his money belt.

Scott shook his head. "You can get the next one."

Gary didn't know how he felt about Scott paying for him, but the pleased and proud look on Scott's face silenced his protests. "Thank you." Scott had planned this and the devious smile on his face only confirmed it.

Scott nodded and got up. "We should get some food before we're left behind." They ate in relative haste and then hurried down the stairs to disembark from the first deck.

The ship looked massive as Gary gazed up at it from the outside. Tom set a hurried pace as they walked down the pier to the Bridgetown Cruise Terminal. They passed through the duty-free shopping area and followed the signs to the tour stops where their tour was already loading onto the bus. Gary showed his ticket and boarded behind Scott. He couldn't see any seats available, until one of the other passengers lowered a jump seat in the aisle and Scott sat down. Then another seat was lowered one row up for Gary. Tom and Bill were behind him and they got the last two seats, officially packing them in like sardines. The door closed and the bus began to move. Thankfully the drive was short, and they arrived at another pier, where his ticket was taken, and they were directed to a pair of tall, sleek sailing catamarans. Following Scott, he boarded and sat next to the big man.

"Everyone, please take off your footwear," one of the crew instructed, as they cast off. "You won't need them, and they'll scuff the deck surface." Gary slipped off his shoes and wiggled his toes. "We're waitin' for another bus, so have a seat and relax, you on vacation!" He smiled a big toothy grin as he sang the last word, and Gary felt himself relax and lean slightly against Scott.

Gary watched as more passengers got on the boat, and his breath caught when he saw Frank standing in line. Before he could say anything, Tom and Bill were on their feet, standing in Scott's line of sight and looking around to the other members of their group. Looks passed from couple to couple and person to person. In an instant Gary saw his fun day with Scott turn into a potential nightmare. Gary saw Sam, always the cop, speaking to one of the crew quite urgently and saw him nodding in return.

As Frank boarded, the man walked up to him and inspected his ticket. "Mon, this is for the other boat. It's right behind this one." He pointed to the other boat, and Gary saw a nearly murderous look on Frank's face as he got off and walked to the other boat. Scott hadn't seen a thing and for that Gary was grateful. He mouthed a thank-you to Sam.

"We have pineapple juice, orange juice, and fruit punch, along with soda and water. Alcohol will be served after we're done snorkelin'. All drinks are included, and we'll pass out all the equipment as we get closer, so sit back and relax. We're gonna have a good time." The boat began to move, and they motored out of the harbor before pulling up the sails and cutting the engines.

Gary and Scott took turns slathering sunscreen on each other as the wind took over and their trip got much quieter. Water bounced against the hull, and fruit drinks and soda flowed, along with homemade cookies and banana bread. The lush Barbadian coast passed by as they sailed out and anchored in Turtle Bay. Gary put on his snorkel and mask, along with an inflatable buoyancy vest. Scott got his vest tangled, and Gary helped him straighten it out. "Don't we get fins?" Gary asked one of the guides.

"No, mon, they scare the turtles."

Gary followed Scott down the front swim stairs and into the warm, almost soft water. When the group was together, the guide led them a short way from the boat and threw some bait into the water. "It's a little murky today, so be patient," he yelled to the group.

Gary floated near Scott and looked down through his snorkel into the cloudy blue water. Unfortunately, there was nothing to see. A large piece of the bait floated by, and Gary pointed it out to Scott. They stayed together and watched.

Soon a dark shape materialized from the bottom. At first it just looked like a blob, but as it got closer, a head and legs could be seen. The turtle glided to the bait, biting off a chunk. Gary was about three feet away. He glanced over at Scott, who pointed back to the turtle. He felt a hand on his leg, stroking his skin as they watched the turtle feed and glide through the water. He must have been more than two feet across and paid them no attention as he finished off the food and then slowly disappeared into the deep.

Gary surfaced and spit out his snorkel. "That was amazing."

Scott pulled him closer, their vests keeping them afloat. "I'm glad we saw it together."

They spent the rest of their time looking. A school of fish swam by and so did a shark-like tarpon, but they didn't see any more turtles. When the call came up to board, they swam back to the boat with huge, amazed smiles on their faces.

"Did you see turtles?" the captain asked, once everyone boarded. Most people had, but many didn't get a good look. Gary and Scott kept quiet about their sighting, looking at each other and smiling.

The crew pulled up anchor as the other catamaran arrived, and Gary felt Scott tense. He followed Scott's gaze to where Frank was standing on the deck.

"How does he keep finding me?" Scott asked.

Gary watched Scott as they traveled away from the other group and up along the coast. They dropped anchor in another bay. "There are three shipwrecks," the guide said, pointing out over the water. "Each of the dark spots is a wreck. We'll be here for an hour, so paddle around, and have a good look. Do not touch or disturb the wrecks. While you're in the water, we'll be getting your lunch ready."

Gary and Scott spent the hour together, gliding over the wrecks and pointing things out to each other. It was such fun. After snorkeling, the bar opened, lunch was served, and it turned into a party, which was only blotted when Scott kept looking over at the other catamaran.

"Don't let him ruin your fun."

Scott pulled his eyes away from the other craft, and Gary felt them slide over him. "You're right; let's enjoy ourselves." Scott led

Gary to the buffet. Gary knew Frank was still watching, and he could tell that Scott was aware of it too. He just wished the man would move on and leave Scott alone, but he knew that would be too easy.

Chapter 9

"WHAT are you doing today?" Sean asked as Gary sat down to breakfast. Scott was still filling his plate, and Gary's was already heaped with food. They'd both really worked up an appetite.

"I hadn't made any plans." Since he'd joined the party relatively late, he hadn't really given a lot of thought to what he was going to do at each port of call. He'd worked hard to get ahead right up until the day before they were going to leave.

"St. Lucia is supposed to have some lovely beaches. Sam and I were going to look around town and then catch a cab to a beach. You're welcome to join us." Phillip and Scott sat down with their plates and began to eat. "We could all share a cab if you'd like."

Gary looked to Scott, who smiled his acceptance between bites, his hand squeezing Gary's thigh gently. "That'd be great. Are you going to join us?" Gary looked at Phillip, who'd just finished taking a big bite of bagel.

Phillip chewed and swallowed. "Sure, sounds good. Where's everyone else anyway?"

"Mark and Tyler already headed out. I think they needed some alone time," Sam said as he sipped his coffee. "Lonnie and Cory told us about the beach. They, Dan, and Gene were going to head over as well."

"What if Frank shows up?" Gary didn't want to mention him, but it had to be asked.

"When I spoke with Lonnie, he said this was an out-of-the-way beach, so unless he follows us, we should be fine. I'll keep an eye out, don't worry." Sam was ever the cop.

They finished breakfast and agreed to meet at the Internet café at nine. Gary and Phillip hurried back to their cabin to pack their things. "We can both pack in my bag. It'll be one less thing to carry," Phillip said.

"Thanks, Phillip." Gary grabbed what he needed and stuffed his things in alongside Phillip's.

"I'm glad you found Scott. You seem, I don't know... happier." Phillip opened the door, and they hurried down the passageway.

"Have you met anyone?" Gary inquired as they walked.

Phillip shook his head. "No, one shipboard romance is enough. This isn't the Love Boat, after all." They both laughed as they entered the café. Quite a group had already assembled. To Gary's surprise, Mark and Tyler had decided to join them as well. As a group they made their way down the stairs, descending to the first deck and disembarking.

The heat hit them hard. Gary pulled out an old hat to cover his head as they walked down the pier and through the group of shops. "Shopping or beach first?" Lonnie asked as he hailed two taxis.

They shopped first, and then hailed two more taxis to haul them and their purchases to the beach. Gary hadn't spied Frank, but kept his eyes open. Fifteen minutes later, they arrived at a small cove with white sand, lush points framing the bay, tall palm trees, and colorful umbrellas. Small resorts, a few bars, and restaurants lined the sand alongside crystal blue water. Gary rented chairs and an umbrella for the three of them. Phillip wanted to get a tan, while Gary knew he needed to stay out of the sun; he'd had enough yesterday.

Gary watched as Scott pulled off his shirt, his fingers itching to reach out and touch like he had for the last two nights. He reached into Phillip's bag. "Would you like some sunscreen?" Scott nodded and sat at the foot of Gary's chair. With a smile Gary popped the top and began rubbing lotion on Scott's skin. "This needs to be done very thoroughly."

"It does, huh?" Scott asked, as Gary's fingers skimmed along his side.

"Oh, yes." Gary kept working in the lotion, taking his sweet time, his fingers gliding over Scott's broad back and round shoulders. He felt himself getting excited, but no one could see, so he let things happen and went with the feeling.

"I think it's my turn," Scott said softly, and they traded places, with Scott pulling off Gary's shirt before he began rubbing in the lotion. There were few people on the beach and Lonnie had directed them to a rather secluded spot, so Gary wasn't concerned when Scott's hands began to wander. His back was coated, his shoulders and arms, then Scott reached around him and began rubbing lotion on his chest. It felt so good Gary almost began to purr.

"Hey, guys, you have an audience." Bill's voice whispered from the next chair.

Gary immediately began looking around, thinking Frank had somehow found them, but Bill tilted his head toward an umbrella, and Gary saw two men, both of them probably in their seventies, raise their glasses to them as they smiled.

"Hey!" Bill started as Tom walked up to him, his suit dripping on his lover. "I wasn't ready to get wet yet." His protest was silenced when Tom whispered something to him, patting his thigh adoringly.

"You will now," Tom said. "I just rented a couple wave runners. We have them for the next hour and a half. The guy gave me a deal, so we can take turns." Tom turned to Gary. "Why don't you two lovebirds take one out while I take Bill for a spin? We can come back in half an hour and let the other guys have a go."

Tom handed them life jackets and led them to the wave runners. The man showed them how to operate them, then Gary climbed on one behind Scott, and they took off. It felt incredible skimming over the water, spray bouncing up as they skipped from one wave to the next.

"God, this is fun!" Gary shouted, and Scott nodded his head as they slowed down. "How fast are we going?"

"Thirty-five," Scott shouted over the engine. Gary scooted closer, holding tight as they took off again, bouncing and swirling on top of the waves. When they thought their thirty minutes was up, they made their way in. Sam got on with Sean right behind him. Gary and Scott stood in the waves and watched as they zipped away.

Gary felt a hand on his butt, and then Scott was pulling him closer. The waves lifted them and then set their feet back on the sand. There were too many people around to do anything, but Gary was painfully hard inside his suit, and he could feel Scott's arousal as well. He wished they were alone so he could pull off his suit and climb the big man's body. Gary had been wondering what it would feel like to have Scott inside him. He'd almost asked—hell, begged—last night, but Scott had seemed tentative. Gary did his best to push those thoughts from his mind. Ever since he'd met Scott, he couldn't get enough of the man, and he felt so wanton.

Gary felt Scott leading them into deeper water and the waves continued rolling around them. Lying back, he floated on the surface, his body rising and lowering in the passing swells. This was absolute heaven.

His thoughts and contemplation were interrupted by the approach of one of the wave runners. Bill and Tom approached the beach. "Who's next?"

Dan and Gene waded into the water, life jackets dwarfed by their powerful physiques, particularly Gene. Boarding the watercraft, Gary heard them shout their thanks to Tom and Bill before zooming away. "How did you meet those guys anyway?"

Scott was treading water near where Gary was floating. "When I got out of prison, I didn't know where to go. The state paid me some money for my wrongful imprisonment, and since I grew up outside Harrisburg, I returned there to be near my dad. I managed to get a job at a grocery store and found a small apartment, but I didn't know what to do with the money. When I joined the gym near the store, I met Lonnie, Dan, and Gene. They work out together, and Lonnie talks to everybody. He told me he could help manage the money for me, and I made an appointment."

"What'd he say when you told him what happened?"

Scott smiled. "Things that would make most prisoners blush." He began to laugh outright. "Lonnie has a colorful vocabulary. We call them Lonnieisms." Gary had definitely heard some of the

Lonnieisms already. Scott kept laughing. "Anyway, I explained what happened, and he believed me, helped me set up an account to manage my money, and recommended a lawyer who could help me sue that police department and the state."

Gary watched as Lonnie got up from his lounge chair and walked into the water. Scott waved, and Lonnie made his way over. "He's really helped me get used to life on the outside again. Dan and Gene too."

"Hi, birdgazers, you having fun out here?" Lonnie called, and Gary figured that was one of the Lonnieisms Scott had referred to.

"We're fine, Lon. You and Cory having a good time?" Scott replied.

"Perfect—warmth, sand, no phones. It's heaven. Are you guys about ready for lunch?"

"I am," Gary answered and yelped slightly when he felt Scott's hand on his butt, squeezing him a little. Then he relaxed and let Scott support him in the water; it was nice. "As soon as the wave runner rentals are up, we should go eat."

Lonnie nodded his agreement, and they watched as the two runners played out in the bay.

After they turned in the wave runners, they found a beachfront restaurant that specialized in local food and had a veritable feast. After lunch Scott and Gary spread out in the shade of their umbrella, and Gary found himself nodding off, the sound of the waves along with Scott's hand rubbing his back quickly lulling him into a contented cat nap.

When it was time to leave, they gathered their things, and their cab drivers returned to take them to the ship. The drive was quick and noisy, with all of them recalling their beach day. Thank-yous were expressed to Tom and Bill for the wave runners, and to Lonnie for his unexpected lunch treat.

They arrived at the St. Lucia pier, and Gary followed Scott as they lined up for the security check.

"Could you step aside sir?" The guard said to Scott, and a man who looked like a policeman approached. Gary saw Scott turn to him and the look on his face made Gary want to scream. Scott's shoulders hunched and the eyes that had been glowing with fun and excitement turned toward the ground, and his hands immediately clasped behind his back. He looked like a prisoner again. Scott stepped out of the line and was led to a small building, Gary followed behind him along with Sean and Sam. The others were already farther down the pier.

"We got a report from another passenger that a man fitting your description was a convicted felon." The officer checked Scott's identification. "You'll need to come with me so we can check this out."

"But the ship leaves in an hour," Gary said, suddenly very worried.

"I have documentation of my exoneration in the safe in my cabin." Scott's voice, which over the last few days had begun to laugh with joy, suddenly sounded small and quiet again. "It's in the safe." Scott told Gary the code.

"I'll go get them." Gary took Scott's sea pass, and Scott told him the combination. "I'll be right back."

"We'll stay with him."

"Thanks, Sam," Gary said as he took off down the pier, running as fast as his legs could take him. As he approached the ship, there was a line of people embarking. Gary excused himself and explained to one of the cruise officials what he needed. They opened the line and let him through. He hurried through the metal detectors and raced up the stairs. By the time he reached the tenth deck, he was out of breath. Hurrying down the gangway, he reached Scott's cabin and opened the door. Opening the closet, he pushed in the code and the safe just beeped at him.

"Goddamn it! Open you fucking thing!" He pushed in the code again, and this time it whirred, and the door opened. Looking inside, Gary saw a manila envelope. Opening it he saw what looked like official papers. Leaving the safe open, he hurried outside and back down the stairs. At the gangway they didn't want to let him out, but Gary pushed past them and hurried down the gangway, ignoring their calls.

The ship's whistle blew a loud blast, and Gary knew it was the first warning and that he needed to hurry. He could barely breathe as he approached the pier entrance and handed the envelope to Scott, who opened it and took out some papers before handing them to the officer. He looked them over and looked at Scott, then back at the papers, and at Scott's passport.

"I'm sorry to detain you, sir." He handed everything back to Scott. "You're free to go."

Gary wanted to whoop, but he was still huffing as the four of them walked down the pier toward the ship. Gary had some difficulty because of the way he'd left, but Sam helped explain, and they were allowed to enter. The gangways were pulled in after them, and the ship's doors clanged closed as they pushed the call button for the elevator. When the doors opened, they got in.

"I'm going to kill that Frank when I see him," Gary said.

Sam put his hand on Gary's shoulder. "You stay away from him and let me handle it." Gary looked at Sam's face and couldn't suppress the shiver he felt run down his spine.

Gary looked around and saw that everyone was staring at Sam, wondering what he had in mind, but Scott was the first to speak. "I appreciate that you're willing to stand up for me, but it isn't necessary. I don't want anyone getting in any trouble because of me. He's not going to change his mind about anything, and none of you should get involved." Gary watched as the elevator door opened to let people on. Scott stepped out and shuffled away, eyes to the floor.

Gary rushed to catch up. "Scott, wait." The doors closed behind him.

He whirled around. "I need to be alone right now." Another elevator door opened, and Scott stepped inside. Gary debated what he should do and jumped into the elevator as the door was closing. "Gary, I said I needed to be alone." There was no fight or heat in his words, and Gary knew he'd made the right choice.

They were alone in the elevator. "I know what your voice said, but your eyes said you were lonely and feeling a little vulnerable." As the elevator lifted, the glass walls twinkled with the lights of the promenade. Gary moved closer. "You aren't alone, and you don't need to face this alone. What happened wasn't fair, and it wasn't your fault."

"I know that, but I don't want to put anyone else in harm's way, least of all you or your friends."

Gary moved even closer. "They're my friends," he said, running his hands across Scott's cheek, "and you mean something to me, so you mean something to them." For the first time in his life, Gary had friends he knew would be there no matter what, and he could barely believe he'd only known most of them for a little over a month. "Sam knows what he's doing. He's a cop and one of the strongest men I've ever met. He won't do anything to hurt anyone, but he won't let anyone else be hurt either. It isn't in his nature."

The doors opened on Scott's deck, and they got off, walking down the passageway. Scott wasn't talking and seemed to be retreating into himself. At his door, Scott inserted his card in the lock and went inside. Without waiting for permission, Gary followed. He was determined to take silence for a yes, at least this time.

Scott flopped onto the bed, and Gary sat next to him, his hands rubbing small circles on Scott's back. As he did, he felt muscles contracting and relaxing quickly, Scott's shoulders flexing up and down, and Gary realized that Scott was crying. Figuring he needed to let it out, Gary sat where he was, rubbing Scott's back as he let out what Gary figured he'd been holding inside for years. The accusation, trial, imprisonment—through it all, Scott had had to be strong, and he could never let anyone see any weakness while he was in prison.

Suddenly Gary stopped rubbing Scott's back. Looking down at the prone figure on the bed, he felt honored and, in that second, closer to anyone than he'd ever been in his life, even his parents. Scott letting his feelings show in front of him like this was an incredible act of trust. Gary slipped his hand beneath Scott's shirt and rubbed the smooth skin tenderly, letting Scott know he was there.

"What did I ever do to deserve this?" Gary looked and saw Scott's face turned toward him, eyes overflowing. "I didn't hurt that girl, and I went to prison for it. I didn't kill her, and I'm being blamed for her death and punished for it."

"I know it sounds simple, but Frank or anyone else can only hurt you if you let them," Gary said, placing his hand over Scott's heart "He can play his petty games, but they're only effective if you let them be."

Scott wiped his eyes, looking confused.

"Sam knows what to do, and he'll help with Frank, but whatever that guy does is petty and only hurts if you let it. How happy do you think he'd be if he knew how upset you were?" Gary kept rubbing Scott's back, not wanting to break the contact between them.

"So what do you suggest?" Gary felt Scott relax against the mattress, and his tears seemed to have stopped.

"I say we change into bathing suits and make our way to the pool deck. They have live music, and we can swim and soak in the hot tubs, maybe take a sauna or steam afterward."

Gary saw Scott turn his head back toward him. "Act like nothing's wrong? That's your solution?"

Gary shrugged. "It's either that, or stay in here until the cruise is over." Gary leaned closer. "That has its appeal too." Gary began sucking on one of Scott's earlobes and got a low chuckle in return.

A knock on the door interrupted them. Scott sat up and wiped his eyes while Gary answered the door, peeking through the peep hole in the door. He saw Dan standing in the passageway. Gary opened the door and ushered Dan inside.

"I heard what happened." He stepped inside and sat next to Scott. "Are you okay?"

"Yeah, I will be. Gary and I were about to go up to the pool deck. I'm not going to let Frank win." Scott smiled a half-smile, which was a definite improvement.

"Good. Gene and I were going to do the same. We'll probably see you up there." Dan got up and smiled at Gary as he headed to the door. "I saw Bill a few minutes ago, and he said that he was planning a surprise party for Tom tomorrow night and asked all of us to join them."

"Tom's turning fifty. Can you believe it?" Gary supplied.

Dan opened the door. "I hope I look that good when I turn fifty." He opened the door and left the room, closing it behind him.

"So, Big Man, are you gonna change or what?" Gary sat on the edge of the bed and watched as Scott got up and opened his suitcase.

"What are you doing?" Scott asked as he pulled out his bathing suit.

"I intend to watch." Gary sat back, his eyes riveted on Scott as clothing began to disappear.

"Okay, but you have to return the favor," Scott replied, and Gary had no problem with that.

Chapter 10

THE walk up the pier felt like skipping on air. They'd had one hell of a great day on Antigua. A small van had picked them up at the base of the pier and whisked them off to the other side of the island. They'd transferred to small boats, where they sped out to a secluded, shallow cove. Then they changed to kayaks and spent an hour paddling around the cove. Mangroves lined the shore, and starfish and small coral lined the bottom, with jellyfish and other sea creatures skittering along in the water beneath them. He and Scott had shared a kayak, and they took turns pointing out things to see. The sun, the breeze, the water, and the peace all combined so that, by the time they were done, they were tired and completely relaxed. The boats had picked them up again and taken them to small islets where the Caribbean met the Atlantic. These coral islands were covered with cactus, battered, and buffeted by the waves until some of the islands had holes in them, worn right through the rock.

At one of the larger islands, the group put to shore. Gary and Scott climbed the rocky path to the top of the island, where the wind blew around them, and the sound of the waves could be heard crashing against the rocks below. They were alone, and Scott pulled him close and kissed him hard, saying nothing. There was no need for words; Mother Nature provided more inspiration than mere words could ever hope to. The sound of others approaching broke them apart, but they stood close together and looked out over the waves until the guides called them back.

Then they were in the boats again, going the short distance to an anchorage. They donned snorkels and masks and slipped carefully into the water. Below them was another world. A variety of coral spread out as far as they could see. Mounds that looked like brains, wispy fans swaying back and forth in the waves, tubes and spikes of yellow, orange, and brown, all passed under them as they kicked through the water. Fish of every color imaginable swam by, ignoring them completely. Gary felt Scott behind him, tapping on his leg. Looking quickly he saw Scott point as a small octopus skittered to its hiding place in the coral. It was wonderful, almost magical, and Gary was happy that he got to experience all this with Scott. In the quiet, he started to worry about what would happen at the end of the week when they'd both have to go home. But that was later. Right now he could see Scott's bathing-suit-covered butt ahead of him, and he paddled toward it.

A whistle called them back to the boats and the trip to home base, where they were served rum punch and then taken back to the van and driven to the pier.

"Did you enjoy the trip?" Gary asked, as he found himself bounding along the pier, his arms swinging.

"Very much," Scott answered, bumping his hips into Gary's. There hadn't been any sign of Frank all day. Gary knew it was hopeless to believe he might have given up on his obsession with Scott, but he was grateful for the reprieve. They had no issues with port security, and entered the ship to find Bill waiting for them.

"Don't forget, we meet in Portofino at six forty-five. Tom has no idea and thinks we're having dinner together at seven."

"We'll both be there, don't worry." Gary had done some shopping and found a small gift for Tom, much to his relief. Gary was thrilled that he'd been invited and was even happier that Bill had extended an invitation to Scott and their new friends—Lonnie, Cory, Dan, and Gene. Gary was coming to realize that he was lucky enough to have found some of the nicest people possible for friends.

The elevator arrived and took them to Scott's deck. "What are your plans for the rest of the afternoon?" Scott asked a little tentatively. Gary turned toward him and smiled as they walked down the passage and into Scott's cabin. As soon as the door closed, Gary was all over him. He heard a rumbly laugh deep in Scott's chest. "I guess I have my answer."

"You better believe it." Gary began climbing the big man. "More kissing, less talking." The laugh ceased, and Scott picked Gary up and carried him the step to the bed, placing him on the mattress. Gary got what he wanted: less talk, more kissing, and everything else.

Sated, they made their way to a late lunch and then spent the late afternoon on the pool deck. Gary dozed off in one of the deck chairs and woke to Scott's soft lips brushing over his cheek. "We should think about going in. You're gonna get burned."

"If I do, will you rub lotion on me?"

Scott's hand rested on the small of Gary's back, and he moaned very softly, wishing that hand would go lower. "I'll rub lotion on you anyway." Gary got up and grabbed his towel. "Where are you going in such a hurry?"

Gary leaned close. "Where we can put those hands of yours to much better use." Gary saw Scott's eyes widen, and then he was on his feet as well, walking right behind him. Gary could almost feel Scott's eyes on his back, and without looking, he walked to Scott's cabin.

The rest of afternoon flew by in a flash of passion. Before dinner Gary found himself back in his and Phillip's cabin. It felt so strange, almost like he was in the wrong place. He hadn't realized he'd spent so much of the cruise sleeping in Scott's cabin that his own felt strange. After cleaning up, he changed and bantered back and forth with Phillip. He was happy, very happy.

"Have you and Scott talked about what happens after the cruise?" Phillip sat on the edge of his bed, looking at Gary as he finished dressing.

That was the last thing Gary wanted to think about right now. He'd been thinking about it every time he let his mind wander. "No. There isn't really a point, is there? He lives in another part of the country." Gary finished knotting his tie and looked in the mirror.

"Is that what you want? A short fling and then you both go your separate ways?"

Gary was instantly offended and glared at Phillip until he saw his expression and realized he wasn't being judgmental. "No. I just don't know what else is possible. We'll only have known each other for a week, and it really isn't practical to move to another state after just a week." Gary hated the thought of going home without Scott, but he didn't know what other options there were. Thankfully Phillip left it, and they finished getting ready for Tom's birthday dinner.

The Italian restaurant on board was simple and elegant, with low lighting and a romantic atmosphere. A large table had been set up, and the hostess ushered them to it. He and Phillip were the first to arrive, and Gary looked back at the door as Scott walked in, looking incredible in his dark suit and white shirt. This was a man built to wear clothes, with his broad shoulders and narrow waist. Scott walked over and sat next to Gary, holding Gary's hand beneath the table.

Bill had obviously been planning, because each place had been set with chocolates and black party favors. The waiter approached and filled their water glasses as Mark, Tyler, Dan, and Gene arrived, followed a few minutes later by Lonnie and Cory. The conversation built as Sam and Sean joined the party as well. Gary kept checking his watch and looking toward the door. He saw Frank walk into the restaurant and tensed as he began walking toward their table.

Scott stood up, and Frank glared at him as he approached. "Sir, do you have a reservation?" the hostess inquired, and Frank stopped walking and turned to her. Gary couldn't hear his response, but he heard the hostess's, "I'm sorry, but we're booked for the evening." Frank glared at Gary, and he felt a shiver run along his spine. "That's all right. I just want to speak to my friends a minute," he said, loud enough for Gary to hear, and then he began to make his way toward the table. Fuck, the man was pushy as hell.

Gary looked at a very pale Scott and then turned back to Frank, trying to figure out how to keep him away. "This is a private party, and you're not invited." He turned toward the hostess. "This man isn't with our party." She looked bewildered and unsure of what to do, and thankfully one of the waiters stepped in between them.

"Sir, I have to ask you to leave."

Frank's eyes shot daggers at both him and Scott, and Gary knew Frank was capable of hurting him, but without another word, Frank turned and stormed out of the restaurant, the door banging as it closed.

Gary stared after him for a second before helping Scott back to his seat. He couldn't help wondering what the man hoped to gain. Turning to Scott, Gary saw him put his napkin on the table and push back his chair. "I'm not going to ruin everyone's dinner."

"No one's ruining dinner," Sam said in his firm voice. "You're not responsible for his behavior." Scott looked around the table and slowly lowered himself back in the chair, much to Gary's relief. "I have an appointment tomorrow with someone from the cruise line, and we'll get this cleared up once and for all."

Gary saw Bill and Tom walk into the restaurant, and they all watched the surprise register on Tom's face as Bill guided him over to the table.

"Happy Birthday, Tom!" Bill said and smiled as they approached the table.

"How'd you do all this?" Tom asked, grinning from ear to ear as he looked around the table.

"Sean helped me with the planning and carried all the decorations in his luggage so you wouldn't see them." Tom took his seat with Bill next to him. The waiters opened bottles of champagne and filled glasses, and they toasted to Tom's fiftieth and many more to come. The waiters passed out menus, and dinner began with smiles and happiness. Gary noticed that Scott had begun to smile, and Gary took his hand, holding it as their orders were taken and the party began.

The ship's photographer made an appearance as the wine was being poured and everyone posed for pictures, smiling and wishing Tom all the best. Presents were opened, and Gary breathed a sigh of relief that Tom seemed to like what he'd gotten for him. It wasn't much, just a simple necklace in bamboo with black hematite beads. Gary had signed the card from both him and Scott, to Scott's surprise and obvious delight, judging by the smile and the look he gave Gary, which made him shiver with excitement.

First courses of Caesar salad and mussels appeared, followed by the entrees. The service was wonderful, and they rarely had to ask for anything. Everything just seemed to appear as if by magic. Gary felt Scott's hand on his thigh, rubbing slightly, a huge, relaxed smile on the big man's face. After clearing the dishes, the waiters paraded out a huge cake, setting it in front of Tom.

"We can't provide candles, but we can sing." One of the waiters pulled out a pitch pipe, and after blowing a note, the waiters sang happy birthday to Tom in four-part harmony. When they were done, everyone clapped, and the servers cut the cake.

Gary excused himself and went to find the little boy's room. After finishing, he was washing his hands when a man stepped next to him. "You may think you know him, but you don't."

Gary turned his head and saw Frank standing next to him, his eyes boring holes into Gary. "Like you do," Gary sneered back and quickened his pace.

"Oh, I know him."

Gary reached for a towel to dry his hands, intent on getting away from this creepy person as soon as possible.

"You may think he's some sort of victim, but he's not. He's a criminal who killed my sister."

Gary felt his anger rising. "Scott didn't lay a hand on your sister. He was proven innocent." Gary met Frank's eyes and bored into them with his gaze. "If anything it's your sister's fault. She helped identify the wrong man and sent an innocent person to prison, and if she killed herself, it was probably over guilt."

Gary almost smiled to himself. He actually saw a crack in Frank's armor, like he'd managed to sow a seed of doubt. "You should spend your time finding the man who really attacked your sister instead of hounding Scott." Gary finished up and walked to the door. "Stay away from all of us."

Gary reached to open the door and heard Frank's voice behind him. "Whatever you think, that man in there," he said, pointing toward the restaurant, "is anything but innocent. If you have the guts, ask him about Jimmy Tanner."

Gary stopped and turned. "What about him?"

"Go ahead. Ask your boyfriend, if you have the guts," Frank spat.

Gary was about to leave when Frank pushed by him and left the restroom, the door banging against the stop in his haste. Gary pushed it open again and stepped into the hall, trying not to give anything Frank had said a second thought.

Returning to the restaurant, Gary found everyone where he'd left them, talking and laughing as they ate cake and finished the wine. Gary's gaze inevitably found its way to Scott, and he couldn't suppress a smile when he saw a twinkle and the small smile lines around his eyes. He didn't look like he could hurt anyone. As Gary walked to the table, he wondered how he could find out about this Jimmy person without having to ask Scott about it. He was sure there was nothing to it. Shaking his head slightly to clear away the thought, he joined his friends at the table as another cork popped and everyone clapped and held up their glasses for more champagne and yet another round of toasts. This was a celebration, after all.

Gary took his seat and joined in the fun. "Is everything okay?" He heard Scott's voice in his ear, and he turned to him and smiled.

"Everything is fine. Did I miss anything?"

"Only Tom's thank-you kiss to Bill." Gary turned toward the Scott. "It went something like this." Before Gary could move, Scott was kissing him hard, his tongue sliding into Gary's mouth, the taste of wine, cake, and Scott bursting onto his tongue. A chorus of awww's and laughter pulled them apart, and Gary blushed as he looked around the table.

"No, Scott," Tom said from the other end. "It was like this."

Gary watched as Tom devoured Bill's lips, a hand combing through his lover's hair as the kiss deepened. Then Tom broke away, and Gary looked around the table, noticing that everyone was breathing just a little bit harder, including himself.

"You youngsters certainly don't have a monopoly on passion, you know." Both Tom and Bill began to chuckle. Tom rested his head on Bill's shoulder, whispering something into Bill's ear that made the stocky blond blush slightly.

Tom stood up and raised his glass. "Here's to my B, the love of my life and one of the best people I know. Thank you for making my birthday memorable." Tom raised his glass and everyone followed. "Now that I've reached fifty, I've decided that we're going to start counting backward, so next year I hope you're all around to celebrate my forty-ninth." Tom raised his glass again, and everyone laughed and toasted.

Lonnie stood up to offer a toast. "I've been on close to forty cruises, and who'd have thought a bunch of homos, no offense, could make a vacation the best one I've ever had?" Lonnie smiled as everyone at the table raised their glasses, and then Tom immediately stood back up.

"And who'd have thought a couple of breeders, no offense," Tom said, looking at Lonnie and Cory and smiling, "could be so much fun? Here's to a fantastic rest of the cruise." Glasses were raised a final time and drained. Conversation continued for a while until everyone filtered out of the restaurant and back toward their decks.

Gary felt preoccupied. His mind kept running over Frank's words, and he hated his traitorous brain for it. But that same mind kept reminding him that he hadn't known Scott all that long. Gary's heart and cautious mind warred with each other until they reached Scott's cabin door. Then Scott turned around, and Gary saw those gleaming eyes and that bright smile. His mind short-circuited, and Gary returned the smile. Arms slid around his waist, pulling him closer as the door was opened.

The door clicked closed, and they reached the bed, Scott's lips on Gary's. Gary's jacket and shirt slipped off his shoulders, and his pants slid down his legs. Lying on the bed naked, he watched as Scott stood at the end of the bed performing a magical strip tease in the dimly lit room. Broad shoulders appeared from beneath the shirt and coat, and Gary sat up on his knees on the bed. Scott stepped back so he couldn't touch, but Gary had to get closer. His gaze followed Scott's hands as they slid down his stomach to his belt buckle. Gary heard shoes thunk on the floor, and then the belt opened, followed by Scott's pants. The fabric parted, and Gary leaned closer, watching as Scott turned around and the fabric slid down a dimpled, black-fabric-covered butt.

The sight was too much for Gary, and he pounced as Scott turned around. Scott caught him in his strong arms, a soft chuckle resonating in his chest. Gary wound his legs around Scott's waist, and an arm held him close while a hand supported his butt. Linking his arms around Scott's neck, pressing their lips together hard as his patience ran out, Gary went wild, devouring Scott's lips as he rubbed his aching hardness against his stomach, squirming on Scott's hand. Then he was being lowered to the bed, pulling Scott down along with him. Scott's skin against his felt so good, and Gary moaned constantly as his consciousness centered on only them.

"Scott, please," Gary begged as Scott continued kissing him. Scott answered his plea by running his tongue over one of Gary's nipples. "Scott...."

"I'm gonna take my time, Gary," Scott whispered as he blew on the wet flesh, sending shivers up Gary's spine. "It's been a long time, and I want to do this right. You deserve it." Scott's words, deep and low, resonated through his body.

"So do you," Gary murmured as Scott moved his lips to the other nipple, treating it to the same delicious torture. Gary vibrated on the bed, trying to squirm away as he thrust his chest against Scott's lips. The sensations were almost overwhelming, and he couldn't quite figure out what to do. Scott's hand slid beneath his back and lifted him up, his head falling back as lips devoured his skin. Gary loved every second of it, and when Scott parted his legs, and his lips trailed down his chest, Gary inhaled deeply in expectation. He wasn't disappointed when Scott lapped his tongue down Gary's cock before opening his mouth and sliding his lips down his length. Gary could barely breathe as he was surrounded by hot wetness. Up until now, they'd taken it slowly, but Gary was starting to come unglued, and he began to thrust his hips.

"That's it, take what you need." Scott's voice resonated as Gary once again felt Scott's lips on him. He couldn't control his hips, thrusting and moaning as Scott met each movement. He felt his excitement build deep inside, and Scott sucked hard, pulling his climax from him. With a groan, he came, lights flashing behind his eyes as he emptied himself, gasping for breath.

Gary collapsed back on the bed, completely spent, and Scott reclined next to him, kissing him hard. He could taste himself on Scott's lips along with Scott's own unique flavor. He felt Scott reach to the nightstand and heard the snick of a bottle opening. Gary lifted his legs and warm fingers tickled his opening before slowly pressing inside.

Gary's breath caught as a long digit slid into his body. "Scott…." It felt overwhelming, and when Scott bent his finger slightly, a zing of pleasure shot through Gary, and his breath whooshed from his body. Scott waited and then repeated the movement, rubbing the spot again and again. A second finger joined the first, and Gary rocked his head on the pillow. "Please don't tease me."

Scott's fingers slid away, and the bed shifted as Scott knelt between his legs. A packet ripped, and a few seconds later, Gary felt Scott press into him. Gary steadied his breath as Scott slid deeper into his body until he felt Scott's hips against his butt. With a deep sigh, Scott brought their lips together in a searing kiss as he began to move in small, slow movements.

Gary held Scott tight, kissing him back, and Scott began thrusting longer and deeper. "Feels so good, Gary, so hot." Scott pulled back, placing Gary's ankles on his shoulders, and then he slid back inside in one long, fluid movement. Gary groaned loudly as their bodies rejoined.

"Yeah, Scott, take me." Gary was hard as a brick even though he'd come not ten minutes earlier, and Scott began driving into him long and hard, pulling out completely and then drilling back into him. Their groans and moans filled the cabin and their movements timed themselves to the gentle rocking of the ship.

Scott's movements became ragged and his thrusts deepened. Gary found himself gripping the bedding in his fists as Scott drove deep, groaning in a rumbling, resonant tone. Gary felt him throbbing deep inside him, and the last of his control snapped as he came on his chest, Scott's hand joining his own on his cock.

Holding each other loosely, their breathing evened out and the gentle rocking that had accompanied their passion now lulled them to sleep.

Chapter 11

GARY woke later to the feel of the ship rocking and Scott's arms wound tightly around him. His mind wouldn't settle, and he found himself staring at the ceiling, his mind refusing to shut down enough to let him sleep. *Jimmy Tanner.* The name kept reverberating through his brain. Gary didn't want to give any credence to anything this Frank guy had said. Scott snuffled and pulled him closer, wisps of his long hair tickling Gary's shoulders.

Whatever had happened was over a long time ago, and Scott wasn't the same person he was then. Gary kept telling himself to let it go. His heart told him he'd be better off, but his head refused. "Go to sleep, Gary," Scott muttered sleepily as a big hand rubbed small circles on his stomach. "Whatever it is, will still be there in the morning."

Scott was right, and he couldn't find out anything anyway, not on the ship, so he might as well give it up. It wasn't important enough to ask Scott, so it wasn't important enough to worry about. With his mind made up, Gary settled and closed his eyes, drifting into sleep.

He woke happily, a hand sliding along his cock and lips nibbling his ear. "Scott," Gary chuckled as he was rolled onto his back, Scott's weight pressing him against the mattress. "Is this your idea of a wake-up call?"

"You're complaining?" Scott's eyes glistened as he leaned closer, nibbling Gary's neck.

"Good God, no." This was the best way to wake up ever, and Scott made good and sure that absolutely everything was awake.

Afterward they both fell back to sleep, only waking when the phone rang. "Are you two coming to breakfast?" Phillip teased.

"We'll meet you there in half an hour," Gary said before hanging up. "I guess we're being summoned." Scott's stomach rumbled loudly, and Gary grinned. "And not a moment too soon." After another kiss, they both got up. Gary began getting dressed while Scott cleaned up, and then he took his turn in the bathroom.

Once they were dressed and ready, they left the cabin. Gary turned the wrong way and walked to the forward elevators, where he found himself outside the ship's Internet café. Without pausing, he called the elevator, and they went up to breakfast, but the seed had been planted.

After breakfast everyone was going to St. Maarten for the day. They decided to share a cab to Orient Beach and had agreed to meet in an hour. Gary needed to pack his things, so he and Scott were going to meet with the other guys and head off the ship.

The elevators were jammed, so Gary took the stairs and found himself back outside the Internet café. "It won't hurt to put this to bed," he sighed to himself as he sat down at a terminal and swiped his sea pass.

He brought up Google and entered the name Jimmy Tanner, getting the requisite million hits. He tried James Tanner and got nearly the same number. Knowing he needed to narrow the search, he tried "Jimmy Tanner inmate" and got a small number of hits. Gary clicked on the second entry and found an article about a young man who'd been killed in prison in Pennsylvania. "Holy crap!" The man had been killed in the same prison where Scott had spent much of his time. He read further.

The article stated that Jimmy Tanner had been killed in an altercation in the prison yard by another inmate. Unfortunately details were sketchy, and Gary pressed the back button to see if he could find anything else. Another entry contained a few more details, explaining that Tanner had been stabbed and that a number of inmates were questioned and that the investigation was ongoing. It certainly wasn't much, but it was enough to get Gary wondering. He felt fairly certain that Scott hadn't killed Jimmy, but he couldn't help being curious about what had happened.

Going back to the list, he looked through a few more sites, but nothing seemed pertinent. Logging off the Internet session, he got up and made his way back to his cabin, putting his card in the door.

"Gary, I was wondering where you were. We need to get going." Phillip was a barrel of energy. "Get your things packed so we can leave."

Gary nodded and began getting things together, not really paying attention to what he was doing. His mind was on those articles and the million questions they had raised.

"What?"

"Are you okay?" Phillip asked.

As usual he'd been thinking of Scott and their limited time together. He'd been thinking about that more and more as the cruise wore on. Each day brought them closer to parting, and each day he grew to care for the man more and more. And this stuff with Jimmy Tanner only added to his preoccupation. "Yeah, fine. Why?" Gary forced his attention back to the present.

"You haven't heard a word I said." Phillip began gathering Gary's things for him. "We're going to the French side of the island."

"So?" Gary knew he really needed to pay attention; he'd obviously missed something.

"We're going to a beach that allows nude swimming." Phillip's eyes were whirls of delight.

Gary laughed. "That's fine, but I'm not getting a sunburned butt or bits." He made sure he had a bathing suit. He wasn't so sure he was really interested in seeing his friends naked. It's hard to look at them the same way after you've seen all their bits and pieces. They checked the bag a last time and then left the cabin, meeting the guys at the designated location.

He and Phillip were the last to arrive. They made their way to the gangway and outside into the hot, humid sunshine. At the end of the pier, Tom found a large taxi that agreed to take all of them to the beach.

Gary climbed inside, and Scott slid in next to him. Once everyone was in, the door closed and the driver took off through the heavy traffic. It took about twenty minutes, but they turned in and pulled up to a place called Bikini Beach. "Is everything okay?" Scott asked as they walked to the beach.

"Sure." Gary hoped he sounded convincing. His mind had been on those damned articles the entire taxi trip, and he felt like kicking himself for even looking. Jimmy Tanner didn't necessarily have anything to do with Scott. It was unfortunate, but people got killed in prison. Gary looked into Scott's face and saw the same caring eyes he knew looking back at him, and he realized he was being stupid. He smiled and took Scott's hand as they crossed the sand. "Everything's perfect." No one appeared to care, and they found a pair of chairs and an umbrella with a perfect view.

Gary watched as people walked along the beach, some in swimsuits, some women without tops, and some stark naked. Gary grabbed his suit and looked around for a changing room. "I'll hold up a towel for you." Grateful for Scott's thoughtfulness, Gary pulled off his shirt and dropped his pants behind Scott's towel, quickly pulling on his trunks. "I take it you aren't going naked," Scott said.

"Nope." Gary adjusted the umbrella and settled on a lounge chair, watching as Scott dropped his shorts, revealing his bikini bathing suit underneath. "I take it you aren't up for naked bathing either?" Now *that* was a sight Gary would pay money to see.

"Don't need to. The only one I want seeing me naked is you." Scott smirked, and Gary shivered with excitement and turned so no one else could see just how excited he was getting.

Scott dug the sunscreen out of his bag. "Would you like me to rub some on you?"

Gary rolled over quickly. The one thing he wanted was Scott touching him, and he'd take it any way he could get it. Hands roamed over his back and shoulders and then down his legs. Gary found himself making soft sounds and heard others settling on deck chairs nearby. Turning his head, he saw the rest of the guys picking their chairs and settling themselves under umbrellas. Without thinking, Gary closed his eyes and reveled in the sensations Scott's hands provided, losing himself in the touch. Scott's hands touched his side, and Gary rolled over. Scott began coating his chest, and Gary relished the gentle contact. Then the hands slid away, and Gary opened his eyes, seeing Scott sitting on his lounger.

Getting up, Gary slid behind him, straddling the seat, his legs sliding around Scott, who handed him the lotion. Then he began returning the favor. Gary spread the lotion on Scott's back and let his hands wander to Scott's sides before winding them around his waist. It felt so nice that he let his body relax against Scott's, pressing his chest to Scott's back as he rested his head against the beautiful man's shoulder. "You feel really good."

"So do you, but people are beginning to stare."

Gary moved away and back to his own chair, huffing softly. "There are old naked people running around everywhere with boobs that look like tennis balls in socks but it's us they're staring at." Gary heard Scott chuckling to himself as he reclined back on his lounger, and he continued muttering under his breath.

"You're so cute," Scott said.

Gary stopped muttering and relaxed, watching the waves as people played in the surf. "Bill told me that tonight's the costume party on the ship."

Scott's head lolled in his direction, and his hand rested on top of Gary's. "I didn't bring anything to wear, did you?"

Gary smiled. "Phillip made sure I did. When we get back to the ship, we'll find something for you." Gary looked around and saw Bill on the next lounge. "Scott doesn't have a costume for tonight."

Bill smiled back at him. In fact he looked downright evil. "Have him stop by our cabin. I'm sure between Tom and me we can come up with something." He smiled over at Tom, who looked equally mischievous.

"Do I even want to know?" Scott asked.

Bill grinned back at him. "You'll love it. I promise."

Gary glanced at Scott and saw the intrigued look on his face. He figured if Scott wasn't worried, he wouldn't be, either, so he rested back on the chair and closed his eyes, letting the warmth reach deep inside him. Resting quietly, time slipped away from him, and he felt Scott get up from his chair. A pair of hands slid under his back and legs, and Gary started as he was lifted off the lounger.

"Scott, what are you doing?" He began laughing as Scott carried him closer to the water.

"It's time we went swimming." Scott splashed into the water and kept walking. Soon Gary felt water against his back, and he held on to Scott as the water got deeper, hanging on like a limpet.

"Now that's more like it." Scott held him close as the waves lifted them off the bottom.

It felt nice being in the water with Scott. Hell, everything felt nice when he did it with Scott. Even a trip to the dentist would be pleasant if Scott went with him. "Did you have something special planned?" Gary rested his head against Scott's shoulder.

"Mmm-hmm." Scott's hand slid into Gary's bathing suit, rubbing over his butt, sliding the fabric down his legs.

"Scott, what are you doing?" Gary's suit slipped off, leaving him naked and very excited. Lifting his legs off the bottom, he wrapped them around Scott's body and moaned softly in Scott's ear as he rubbed against his body. "Everyone can see us."

"Yes they can, so you need to be quiet." Scott teased a finger over Gary's opening, and he hitched up against Scott's chest, rubbing his erection over smooth skin.

That was exactly what he needed, and he began to slide slowly up and down. "Feels so good."

"I know it does." Scott pressed a finger inside, and Gary caught his breath as a wave washed over them at the same time.

"And it's going to feel better." Scott rubbed the spot inside him, and Gary began grinding harder.

"What happened to the shy man I met a few days ago?" Gary kept moving, torn between Scott's finger inside and the friction on his cock.

"*You* happened." Scott added a second finger, and Gary rolled his hips, flashes of light going off behind his eyes as he came against Scott's stomach, his face buried against Scott's shoulder to hide his orgasmic bliss. As he came down, Scott slipped his fingers from Gary's body, and Gary lightly bit his shoulder to keep himself from calling out.

"Isn't that special?" an unfortunately familiar voice sneered behind him.

Gary felt Scott tense, and he placed his feet on the sandy bottom. He felt Scott hand him his suit. He slipped it on his legs and, by some miracle, didn't topple over in the surf.

"Are you going to rape him like you did my sister?"

Gary turned around and saw the venomous look on Frank's pinched face. His hate was definitely making him ugly.

Gary could feel the tension rolling off Scott, but knew nothing short of Frank's disappearance could alleviate it, so he simply glared at Frank with contempt for intruding on their happiness.

"I never hurt your sister!" Scott said through clenched teeth. Gary noticed that Scott was glaring back at Frank and not looking down. "I'm sorry your sister was hurt, and I'm sorry she took her own life, but I never hurt her. I've proven that it wasn't me."

Gary marveled at Scott's self-control, because he wanted to haul off and punch the man in the face. Instead he stood next to Scott, glaring back at the man as waves continued breaking around them.

"Maybe you should concentrate on finding the man who really attacked your sister instead of hounding me." Scott continued as he stepped closer to Frank. "If anyone has reason to be upset, it's me. I was wrongly identified as her attacker, and I never hurt anyone!"

Fire raged in Scott's eyes, and Frank actually backed away. For a second Gary thought Scott might have gotten through to the stubborn man.

"You keep telling yourself that, but what about Jimmy Tanner?"

Gary turned to Scott and watched as the fire in his eyes hissed out like someone had thrown cold water on it. Scott's fists clenched and unclenched, and for a second, Gary thought Scott was going to strike the ugly man, then he saw Scott's shoulders slump, and he heard a soft sigh.

Gary seethed at the man standing in front of him. "Why don't you go on with your own life, you sorry excuse for a human being?" Gary had had enough, and he stepped closer to Frank. "He's done nothing to you except serve time for something he didn't do." Gary clenched his fist, pounding the surf around his waist. "So just back off and stay away before I pound you like the little worm you are!" Frank backed away and began looking around.

"Gary."

"Go on before I beat the hell out of you!" He punched the water and glared at the man as Frank started to step back toward the beach. What the fuck was wrong with the man anyway? They had to find a way to keep Frank away from Scott. He was starting to think that Frank wasn't just angry, but obsessed. The thought made him angrier. Scott sure as shit didn't deserve that.

"Gary." He turned and saw Sam standing next to him. "Let him go." He watched as Frank stormed along the beach, picking up an empty beach chair and tossing it aside.

"I intend to. I just want him to stay away from Scott." Gary looked toward their loungers. "Where is he?"

"That's what I've been trying to tell you. Scott's gone." Gary ran toward their lounges. Scott's bag was gone along with his towel. "He raced toward the parking lot."

Gary took off, running around the building and into the driveway. All he could see were a few cab drivers standing around lounging against their vehicles, but Scott was nowhere to be found. "Have you seen a big man with long, black hair?"

"Yes, he leave in a taxi a few minutes ago. You want to follow?" The dark man's face brightened at the prospect of a fare.

"He needs to be alone, Gary." He turned toward Sam's voice. "You can talk to him when we get back to the ship." Gary felt himself deflate, and he shook his head at the driver and let Sam lead him back to the beach. He slumped on his lounge chair and withdrew into a book he'd brought along. After reading the same page multiple times, he put down the book and stared out over the water.

As beautiful as it was, he didn't want to be there anymore. The guys got him something for lunch, but he barely noticed what he was eating. Phillip sat next to him and kept comforting him, but nothing was working. In the afternoon he went back to the lounger and stared at the water until the guys told him it was time to leave.

With a sense of relief, he changed and followed them to the van that would take them back to the ship. "It'll be okay, Gary." He nodded an acknowledgement to Sam's attempt at comfort and bounced with the van on the rough roads until they reached the dock. Getting out, he paid his share of the fare and walked quickly up the pier, presenting his sea pass and going through the metal detectors. He climbed the stairs to Scott's deck and walked down the passage, knocking on Scott's door. He got no answer. Knocking again, he waited and then began wandering around the ship, checking the pool deck as well as the gym and promenade, but he could find no sign of Scott. Hell, Gary didn't even know if he was on the ship at all.

Dejected and now more than a little concerned, he made his way to his cabin and found Phillip inside. "Come on, we're going to the gym."

Gary shook his head. "No thanks." He really didn't feel like doing anything right now.

Phillip grabbed his bag and walked toward the door. "We'll be there a while if you change your mind."

"Okay." Gary raised his hand as Phillip left the cabin, leaving him alone. The ship's whistle blew, announcing the last warning, and Gary picked up the phone, calling Scott's cabin, but got no answer. A few minutes later, he heard the horn again, and then the ship began to rock slowly with the motion of the sea.

Chapter 12

GARY had never been one with a lot of patience when he was worried, and things weren't any different now. He had to believe that Scott was somewhere on the ship. He'd noticed before leaving port that they'd sometimes call for people to come forward. Gary assumed it was people who hadn't reboarded the ship. There'd been no announcement this time, so at least Gary had hope. Getting up from his bed, where he'd flopped in frustration, he decided to look again. This was not how he wanted to spend one of their last days together—he wanted to be with Scott.

Leaving his cabin he made his way down a deck to what he remembered was Gene and Dan's cabin. He hoped Scott's friends would know where he was.

Gary knocked on the door and waited. A few seconds later, Gene opened the door.

"Sorry to bother you, Gene," Gary said, "but have you seen Scott? He left the beach early, and I can't find him." Instead of answering, Gene opened the door wider, and Gary saw Scott sitting on the side of the bed with Dan sitting next to him. Both men turned toward him as he entered the cabin. "Are you okay?"

Scott didn't answer, but Dan said something and then got up from the bed. "We'll leave you a while." Dan patted Scott on the shoulder and then ushered Gene from the room, while Gary took his place on the bed next to Scott.

"Is this about the man Frank mentioned earlier, Jimmy Tanner?"

Scott nodded. "I killed him. Well, good as, anyway."

Gary was stunned and sat still, hoping and praying that Scott would continue. "What happened?"

Scott didn't look at him, keeping his eyes pointed at the floor. "In prison, you don't make many friends, and those you do don't stay around for long for one reason or another. But Jimmy was special." Scott heaved a breath and continued. "I'd been inside for almost a year, staying away from everybody and looking as tough as I could. It seemed to work, 'cause everybody left me alone, pretty much. Anyway, Jimmy got transferred from another place and began to talk to me in the yard sometimes." Scott turned on the bed. "He had trouble with one of the other guys. It's hard to explain, but he thought of Jimmy as his personal property to do with as he pleased. As soon as Jimmy arrived, he tried to stake his claim."

Gary wasn't quite sure what Scott was talking about, but he kept quiet, hoping he'd understand, and he didn't want Scott to stop talking.

"Jimmy didn't like it and resisted. Woke us all up screaming 'Leave me alone!'" Scott swallowed hard. "I guess he must have gotten in a few good licks because the next thing I heard was a cry of pain, and the guards came running. Jimmy was okay, and after that we kind of stayed together. There's safety in numbers."

"How long did you know him?"

"We were friends for about four years when someone else decided they wanted to try to lay a claim to him." Scott finally looked at Gary. "I should tell you that Jimmy was really pretty, sort of feminine-looking, which is a curse inside. This time, I stood up with Jimmy, and the guys all thought I already had a claim on him. They left him alone then, for a while."

"What happened?"

"Jimmy and I had an argument about something stupid, and I pushed him away." Scott buried his face in his hands. "When word got around, they started after Jimmy again, and he fought something fierce. This time he didn't win, but he kept fighting and one of his attackers stabbed him with a shiv to keep him from screaming." Scott's shoulders heaved as he tried to keep control of himself. "I was supposed to help keep him safe, and instead I was the one that put him in danger."

"What was the argument about?"

"Jimmy was a thief, and he used to lift things. He couldn't help himself, and he always gave me the stuff back. He always said he wanted to keep his skills sharp." Scott actually lifted his head and smiled. "But this time he dropped and broke a picture of my parents, and I tore into him in front of everyone." Scott began breathing deeply. "It was only a stupid frame, and it cost him his life."

Gary didn't know what to say, but he tried. "Jimmy's death was not your fault. You didn't attack him, and you didn't stab him."

"I know, but I didn't protect him, either." The look on Scott's face was enough to break Gary's heart. Without thinking, he threw his arms around Scott and held him tight.

"You can't do everything." Gary kept holding tightly. "Would Jimmy blame you?"

Scott shook his head. "No." He gulped for air. "I don't think so."

"Then let it go. You can't hold yourself responsible for what everyone else does. I'm sorry you lost your friend." Gary wiped a tear that streaked down Scott's cheek. "You must have missed him a lot."

Scott nodded. "I did. I was alone again and feeling guilty as fuck." He took a deep breath and got up from the bed, and Gary let his arms fall away. "My friends have a way of getting hurt."

"Well, I'm not going anywhere, and I don't think the rest of us are, either." Gary took Scott's hand. "I can't make your memories go away, but I can tell you that you have friends who care about you and that you're worth it."

"Yeah?" Scott's eyes pulled up from the floor. "You really mean that?"

Gary smiled and nodded. "I do. I saw a movie once and it had a great line. 'There's nothing so bad that you can't add a little guilt and make it worse'." He looked up at Scott. "It's okay to mourn your friend. Remember what you liked about him, but don't feel guilty about his death. You didn't kill him."

Scott's head turned to Gary, and he looked as though he could hardly believe what he was hearing. "You're really serious, aren't you?"

"Of course." Gary knew he needed to tread lightly and make sure he picked his words carefully so there wouldn't be any misunderstanding. "You were in prison with the dregs of society, and you had to survive. You didn't belong there." Gary took Scott's hand, running his lips over the knuckles. "You didn't hurt anyone, and the only person responsible for Jimmy's death was the man who slipped a sharpened spoon between his ribs." Gary suddenly realized he'd said too much and let his voice trail off.

Scott's eyes narrowed with suspicion. "How'd you know that?"

"Frank cornered me in the bathroom last night and told me to ask you about Jimmy Tanner." Gary felt like he was walking on egg shells. "I didn't ask because I knew you couldn't have hurt anyone, but I did Google him this morning." He could feel Scott getting ready to bolt again.

"Why didn't you ask me?"

Gary didn't release Scott's hand. "There was nothing to ask about. The articles only said that he was killed, with a brief description of how he died and that the investigation was ongoing. I figured I'd ask you about it later, but then Frank beat me to it." Scott's eyes softened slightly. "Is this a big deal?"

"I guess not."

Gary smiled and kissed Scott's fingers again. "Good, because we have a party to go to, and I'm anxious to see what sort of costume Tom and Bill put together for you." Gary remembered the looks on their faces as they exchanged glances, and he just knew it was going to be something very sexy.

Scott actually smiled.

"I think we should get back to your cabin so Dan and Gene can have theirs back." Gary got up and tugged Scott to his feet. "We need to get ready for dinner and then dress for the party. It should be fun, and I think you need to take your mind off all this for a while." Gary headed for the door. "And if Frank tries anything, it's open season on short, pasty rednecks."

Gary's heart lifted when Scott began to laugh. "It is, huh?"

"Yeah, I'm tired of him being a pain in the ass." They left the cabin, making their way down the passageway. "That reminds me, we need to speak with Sam. He was going to talk to someone from the cruise line about Frank Garrett."

They kept talking until they reached Scott's cabin. "I'll meet you on the promenade in half an hour?"

"Okay." Scott kissed him and then went inside, and Gary made his way to his own cabin. Phillip was already changing, acting even more excited than usual.

"What's gotten into you?" Gary began pulling out his clothes for dinner and put his costume for the party on the bed.

"I have a date." Phillip grinned as he fussed in the closet. "He's joining us for dinner and then we're going to the party together." He pulled out a pair of dress pants and a shirt, holding them in front of him while he looked in the mirror.

"Where'd you meet him?"

"At the beach today. He was lying on the lounger next to me and started up a conversation." Phillip huffed and hung the shirt back up, choosing another one.

"That must have been some conversation."

Phillip put the clothes on his bed and began changing. "It started innocently enough, but progressed pretty quickly after he complimented me on my bathing suit." Phillip stopped moving around like a hummingbird for a second and actually blushed. "Then he complimented me on the way I filled out my bathing suit and asked me if I was going to the party with anyone. He said he'd seen me on the ship with a bunch of guys and wasn't sure if I was with someone."

"Well, at least he has taste." Phillip pinked a little more, and Gary secretly loved it. For the first time, he was seeing a blushing, slightly flustered Phillip. It was almost refreshing. "Remember, I've seen Mr. Happy Pants." Gary laughed as he teased and began dressing. "Scott's is better, but yours is nice too." Gary dodged the pillow that went sailing at his head and they both broke down in peals of laughter as they finished dressing.

"So what's his name?" Gary asked as they left the cabin.

"Dakota." Phillip's eyes sparkled. "He's from Wyoming, and he's a real cowboy on a real ranch and everything."

"Where are you meeting him?"

Phillip checked his watch. "In the Schooner bar in five minutes." Phillip's pace picked up as they reached the elevator and waited for the car.

Getting out on the promenade, Gary went to meet Scott and left Phillip to lasso himself a cowboy. He thought about making a "Yee-hah" sound and waving his hand over his head, but managed to restrain himself. He'd save that for later. Gary found Scott sitting outside the café with a beer on the bar in front of him. Gary sat next to him and ordered a soda.

"Tom just left. He said to stop by their cabin after dinner." Scott gulped his beer. "He had this… look on his face."

"I'm sure it will be fine," Gary said reassuringly, wondering what those two were cooking up. "Don't be nervous." Gary finished his soda, and Scott his beer, before they slid off the stools and wandered through the shopping arcade to the entrance of the dining room.

Dinner was great, and Phillip's date seemed really nice. As soon as they were done, Tom and Bill whisked Scott away to get his costume. Gary and Phillip went upstairs to change into theirs. They'd all agreed to meet on the pool deck near the bar in an hour. They figured the party would be well underway by then.

In the cabin Gary changed into a pirate costume he'd originally worn a few Halloweens ago. It seemed to work and actually still fit. Phillip convinced him to lose the shirt, and he had to admit, it was cooler and sexier. He pushed his self-consciousness aside, and when Phillip was ready they left the cabin to meet their dates.

The pool deck had been set up with a buffet running down one side, lights, and cool Caribbean music. People were already milling around the buffet and standing in small groups drinking and talking. Gary looked for Scott and saw him standing near the bar looking very uncomfortable. Gary kept watching as he approached. "Jesus!" Gary's eyes traveled up and down the man. "You're nearly naked." Scott turned around, and Gary laughed. "A tail and horns?"

"Yeah." Scott blushed profusely and tried to hide behind a pole. "Bill said he wore this a while ago and brought it for Tom."

"I think you look sexy." He did too. Gary let his eyes travel up and down Scott's body. He was barefoot, wearing only a pair of tight, square-cut shorts that were flesh colored. A tail had been affixed to the back and a pair of horns stuck out of Scott's long hair. "Really sexy." Gary had to stop himself from trying to climb the big man, he looked so good.

"But everyone can see my business." Scott stepped out from behind the pole, his hands over his front.

Gary pulled his hands away. "No they can't. It's just a pair of tight shorts." He leaned really close. "But I'll be doing more than lookin' at your business later."

The blush on Scott's cheeks pinked right back up, and Gary smiled. "Come on, let's hit the buffet."

Gary took Scott's hand and led him to the food tables as the music started up again. After they'd eaten a little, Gary and Scott joined the guys by the pool. Sean and Sam were standing close together, moving to the beat of the music. Tom and Bill were doing the same, but Tyler and Mark were actually dancing together.

"Hey, guys." Lonnie and Cory approached with plates in hand. Lonnie had dressed as the Incredible Hulk, complete with green full-body makeup, and Cory looked like a sexy flapper in her fringed dress. Dan and Gene came along right behind them.

"Hi, Lonnie," Scott replied, looking extremely awkward again.

"Good God," Lonnie said, beginning to laugh. "Nice panties, ya birdgazer."

Scott began to laugh as well, looking down at himself. Just then the music changed to a faster beat, and all around the deck couples began to dance. Tom and Bill held each other close, joining Mark and Tyler. Phillip approached with Dakota, dressed as—of all things—a cowboy. Seeing the other couples, they joined in as well.

"You should be ashamed of yourselves." A female voice cut through their fun. "What you're doing is disgusting and an abomination!" Great, it looked like they couldn't have any fun wherever they went—first Frank and now this self-righteous bitch.

Gary was tongue-tied, and the guys stopped dancing, looking embarrassed and uncomfortable. Gary could almost feel the fun being sucked away.

"Look who's talking, you cow." Lonnie stepped up to the woman, getting in her face. "You want to make the world a better place?" The woman nodded without thinking. "Then waddle over to the rail and throw yourself overboard. The world could use one less bigoted moron." She stepped back, but Lonnie kept moving forward. "Better yet, why don't you toddle over to the buffet and eat until you explode."

She'd obviously been taken by surprise, and Gary began to laugh. He nearly doubled over as Lonnie followed the woman across the deck making moo sounds behind her the entire time. The guys started laughing as well and returned to their dancing. Lonnie rejoined the group, taking Cory's hand and joining in the fun. Gary felt a hand on his shoulder and turning around, found himself enveloped in strong arms as Scott pulled him into the dance as well.

He felt Scott's bare skin against his own as they moved. Gary tried to remember that they were standing on the deck and not alone in Scott's cabin, so he pushed his excitement aside, for now, and went with the music. All their friends were doing the same, smiling and laughing as they moved. Being in a group gave Gary a sense of freedom he rarely felt in public. "You're a good dancer," Scott said, his rich voice close to Gary's ear. Gary smiled and held on to Scott as the music continued to pound.

Other couples from around the deck began to gravitate in their direction, joining in the dancing. They just seemed to want to be where the fun was; it didn't seem to matter that they were joining a bunch of men dancing together.

Gary kept dancing, his eyes lingering on Scott before wandering to the people around him. It was then that he saw Frank standing on one of the upper decks, watching them intently. Gary looked back, but said nothing to Scott and just kept dancing. Then he returned his attention back where it belonged. He'd be damned if Frank was going to intrude on their fun. Besides, there were too many of their friends right nearby for Frank to pull anything. Sam would probably rip his head off if he got too close. After a while, Scott stopped and pulled him from the throng. "Are you thirsty?" Scott raised his voice to be heard.

Gary nodded vigorously and followed Scott toward one of the pool bars. He hadn't realized how parched he was until he took a gulp of the soda Scott ordered for him. "That's good." Stepping away from the bar, Scott led them to a quiet spot, and they were quickly joined by some of the guys, who'd also decided to take a break.

"Having fun?" Tom asked as he and Bill joined them.

"Yeah." Gary smiled and tried not to stare at Tom and Bill's outfits, although quite a few others weren't being as polite. They were both dressed in leather shorts, harnesses, and tricep bands with the leather covered in silver studs. "I have to say, it must have been difficult getting that stuff through airport security." Both Tom and Bill laughed, neither of them looking self-conscious in the least. Gary decided that as he approached fifty, he wanted to look as good as these two men... definitely.

"This is great." Gary turned and saw Sam coming from the bar with a beer in hand, looking back toward the dancers. Mark and Tyler were still moving together, completely oblivious to anyone around them. "I spoke to someone today. He's the Master of the Ship and seems to be the law enforcement officer on board."

"What did he say about Frank?" Gary asked hopefully. He was becoming very tired of Frank's stalking.

"I explained what he was doing, but unfortunately, he hasn't really done anything wrong other than being a colossal pain in the ass. I did report what was happening, and the Master said he'd make a record of it."

"Oh." Scott gulped the last of his beer and set down the glass.

Gary saw the disappointment on Scott's face. "Let's not let him ruin the fun, okay?" Scott nodded, and Gary took his hands. "We only have a few more days, and I want to spend them with you." Gary was hyperconscious of the fact that every hour that passed meant less time he had with Scott, and he was becoming more and more determined to make the most of the time left.

Scott set his glass on the bar, and Gary smiled as he followed him to where Mark and Tyler were still dancing. As though they were reading his mind, the musicians began playing something slower. Scott pulled Gary close, his warm skin sliding over Gary's as they moved together to the flowing music. Dozens of other couples did the same around them. Gary looked up and saw Frank still watching them from the upper deck. With his arms wrapped around Scott, Gary smiled up at the obsessive freak, waving at him, and actually saw him pound the railing with his fist before he stormed away. He wondered what the man was planning behind those glaring eyes.

Gary held onto Scott, inhaling his musky scent, feeling his smooth skin against his own. He had to be content with stroking Scott's back, but every now and then, he'd feel Scott's hands slide against his butt, and each time he felt it, Gary had to stop himself from grinding his hard erection against Scott's. He could feel the excitement radiating off Scott's body. The music went on, and they continued moving, Gary making symbolic love to Scott right there on the dance floor. Their hands touched gently as their bodies moved together, and Gary found his focus narrowing to only Scott. When he looked up, he saw only Scott's eyes. When he inhaled, he smelled only Scott's earthy scent of musk and sweat and powerful man.

As a child, his mother had insisted that he learn how to dance. She'd told him it was the best way to express the language of love. Up until now he'd never quite understood, but moving on the deck under the stars with Scott, he suddenly realized what she meant all those years ago. Gary turned his head upward, catching Scott's eyes, and he realized he loved him. The realization took him by such force that Gary swallowed hard and almost stopped dancing. He was in love with Scott.

His first instinct was to tell him, but he couldn't. It wasn't fair. He only had Scott for two more days, and then they both had to go home. Gary leaned his head against Scott's shoulder and moved with him, trying not to let his emotions get the better of him. Besides, just because he was in love with Scott didn't mean Scott was in love with him. So Gary huffed softly to himself and held tight as they continued dancing.

"Do you think we could go back to my cabin?" Scott's rich voice rang in his ears as one was lightly nibbled.

His eyes a little watery, Gary nodded. Scott took his hand and led him across the deck to one of the sliding doors. Frank stood nearby, watching them, and Gary looked up at Scott, who saw Frank as well. Gary saw Scott smile at him and wave. Frank's face pinched further, and he looked about ready to explode.

Scott held Gary close and led them to the elevator. Gary smiled to himself to try to keep from laughing as people stared at the huge, nearly naked man, wearing horns and a tail. "It's not that funny," Scott groused. The elevator doors opened, and Scott hurried them inside. Gary couldn't help giggling, putting his hand over his mouth.

His mirth ceased when he saw another man looking Scott over from head to toe like he was a giant buffet. Gary stared back at the old geezer, and he turned away. When the elevator door opened, Scott rushed them out and along the passageway to his cabin. Opening the door he hustled Gary inside, letting the door close on its own as Gary found himself being kissed until his body felt like it was on fire.

Hands ran through his hair as his lips were taken in a masterful kiss, the pirate hat falling to the floor. Gary felt his knees begin to buckle, but Scott's strong arms held him close, lowering him to the bed. He watched as Scott removed the horns tied to his head and then slipped off the tiny shorts before standing at the foot of the bed in all his naked glory. Gary couldn't stop a breathy moan from escaping as Scott crawled up the bed toward him.

"I want you, Gary. Want to make you beg me to let you come." He took Gary's lips as Gary felt his pants slide away, releasing his erection from the confining fabric.

Gary's breath hitched as he felt Scott's lips surround one of his nipples, tugging on the bud until he thought he'd go crazy. Gary found himself arching into Scott's every touch, his body craving everything he could get. Scott's hands felt so soft, so good... so loving. Gary closed his eyes and let himself believe that Scott felt the same way he did. Every touch sent Gary soaring, and when he felt Scott take him unto his mouth, he could barely breathe.

"Scott." Gary opened his eyes and saw that sexy man taking him deep, those incredible lips wrapped around him. Gary's hips began moving slightly, and Scott lifted his head, bringing their lips together.

"You're the best person I've ever met, Gary." Scott's kiss took Gary's breath away. The big man moved between Gary's legs, spreading them wide. Gary lifted his legs, and Scott's lips slipped from his, moving down his body. Gary held his breath, hoping to feel those lips on him again. Scott's tongue slid down his length and kept going, not stopping until it slid across his opening.

"Scott!" Gary cried out as hot wetness slid over him again and again. The touch was so light, so hot, that he could hardly stand it. His panting breath became more ragged as he felt Scott going deeper, his fingers caressing sensitive skin. "God, Scott." He found himself whining, not sure how to ask for more. Fingers swirled around his opening, teasing the skin, and then slowly, Gary felt a long finger enter him, making small circles. The digit pressed against a spot, *the* spot, deep inside him, and he bucked against the finger, driving it deeper, wanting more. This was Scott, *his* Scott. The realization of his full feelings hit him hard.

His breathing already ragged as he tried to hold onto the last tenuous threads of control, he cried out softly as Scott lifted his head, taking his cock deep between those full lips. Gary threw his head back, crying out again as he came hard, pumping what felt like gallons of himself into Scott.

Gary went completely limp. His entire body was rung out from the most powerful climax he could ever remember. He'd had good lovers before, but none could compare to this, and as he lay on the bed, trying his best to catch his breath, he knew why. There was no doubt in his mind why it had been so good. Gary even opened his mouth to say the words, but Scott's lips were there, tugging on his, hands petting him, loving on him, and deep down, the voice of reason took over, cautioning him. They only had another day together, and then they'd part, probably forever, so Gary held his tongue, swallowing the words as he returned Scott's kiss, pouring everything he felt into his kisses and his touches.

"I want you, Gary, want you so bad." Scott's kisses became ragged, and Gary felt him begin to shake.

Reaching toward the end table, Gary got a condom and pressed Scott back. Using both hands, he stroked Scott's full, hard cock, feeling the throb of its weight against his palms. Tearing open the packet, he rolled the latex down his lover and rested back on the bed. "I want you too."

"Don't want to hurt you." Scott's shaking hand rested against Gary's chest.

He loved that he made Scott this excited, that he made Scott want him this badly. "Won't hurt me, want you now!"

Gary felt Scott press into him, and his breath whooshed out as Scott filled him in a massive thrust, his head hitting the padded headboard with a soft thud. Then Scott pulled back and drove in again, hard and full and thick. Gary watched as Scott thrust his chest forward with each movement, the muscles bulging with strain, dark tresses cascading in front of that handsome face, moving back and forth with each movement. Gary reached up and pushed the locks aside, looking into Scott's lust-filled eyes as the two men moved together in a frantic rhythm fueled by unbridled desire. This was what Gary had dreamed of all his life: someone who could want him with this much intensity. He pushed away the thought that they only had another day together, and rode the waves of ecstasy that he and Scott were creating.

Everything outside of them seemed to narrow and conform to the rhythm of their lovemaking. The rocking of the ship seemed to change so that even the huge vessel wanted a part of it, sharing their passion. The noises in the hall that suddenly seemed so far away all conformed to the rhythm of each of Scott's mammoth thrusts. "I can't get enough of you!" Scott pulled out, held still, and the world seemed to hold its breath until he drove deep inside again, stealing Gary's breath. "Will never get enough of you."

The words came as close to a declaration of love as either of them dared, and Gary's mind flew, pulling him over the edge for the second time in less than half an hour. Panting madly, Gary came again, coating his stomach with his release as he felt Scott thrust deep and then go still, Scott's mouth opening in a silent cry, his body rigid in climax.

Scott collapsed on top of him, going completely limp and gasping for breath. Gary held him close, getting his own breath under control as his hands caressed the muscles of that wide, powerful back. He gasped as he felt Scott slip from his body, feeling a sudden sense of loss. They rested together for a long time, each holding the other silently, skin to skin. Then Scott began to move, slowly getting up and taking care of things before rejoining Gary on the bed.

Snuggling next to him, Scott pulled Gary into a tight embrace, a hand over his chest like a shield. *He doesn't want to let me go, either.* The thought comforted Gary as he felt Scott kiss his neck. Turning his head, they shared a kiss, and then they both curled together, sleep overtaking them way too quickly.

Gary woke some time during the middle of the night. Pushing back the covers, he carefully got out of bed and made his way to the bathroom. After taking care of business, he returned to the room. The first pale light of day peeking around the curtains cast just enough glow that he could see Scott on the bed, his hair cascading everywhere, his face relaxed and beautiful. The covers had been pushed aside, revealing Scott's powerful chest and narrow hips. This man was everything he could want, beautiful on both the outside and inside.

"You're too good to be true," Gary whispered before walking to the bed and climbing back beneath the fluffy coverlet. Scott's arms found him immediately, pulling him close, his eyes never opening. Gary rested still against Scott's body, skin pressing to skin. Taking Scott's hand in his, he lifted it to his lips and kissed his knuckles. He clamped his eyes shut as he wondered how he was ever going to let Scott go. *I spent years looking for someone who makes me feel this way, and now I have to let him go.*

The thought had him blinking back tears, and he couldn't seem to stop them no matter how hard he tried. Wiping his eyes, he got hold of himself and gripped Scott's arm, holding it the way a child might hold a doll.

Gary took a deep breath, releasing it in ragged starts, feeling his emotions just below the surface. "I love you," he breathed softly. There, he'd said it. Even if Scott was asleep, he'd said it. He knew it didn't count, but it was all his aching heart would allow him.

Chapter 13

THEY woke early, and after another round of what Gary could only describe to himself as lovemaking, they agreed to meet for breakfast in the restaurant, and Gary went to his cabin to change, smiling the entire way. When he'd awakened, he'd silently lectured himself that he was going to make the very most of the short time he and Scott had left together.

Sliding his card in the door, the green light flashed, and he entered the dark cabin. He half-expected to see the bed still occupied, but the rumpled covers were empty. He walked to the window overlooking the promenade and reached to pull back the curtains, then felt a thud on the back of his neck. "Jesus Christ!" He whirled around in time to see Frank grab him and start hauling him through the room.

Gary felt his legs get caught in the fallen bedding as he struggled to get his feet under him, and then he was stuffed in the closet. He crumpled in a heap on the shoes and life jackets that covered the floor, holding his aching head, wondering what the hell had happened. He pushed against the door, and it moved slightly before being jammed back in place. There were no latches on the door, so Gary knew that Frank had to be holding it closed. Gary shook his head slightly, and everything he could see started to loop. He stilled and massaged his throbbing temples to stop the world from spinning as the heard the outside door open and quickly close.

Piling the two life jackets on top of one another, he used them as a seat and the spinning seemed to abate. "What are you doing, Frank?" The situation was laughable. "The cabin steward will be here any time to make up the room. What are you going to do, shove him in here with me?"

"I put out the Do Not Disturb sign." He actually seemed pleased with himself.

"And what are you going to do when my friends come looking for me?" Gary held his head and the spinning finally stopped. "What do you hope to gain from this?" Gary figured he could probably push the door open, but wasn't sure if Frank had a weapon, and right now, he figured he was safer from the man on the other side of the door.

Frank didn't answer right away, and Gary hoped he was making the man think, possibly even see how ridiculous the situation was. Then Frank said, "When no one answers, they'll look for you on the ship or think you went to shore."

"Come on, Frank. They know I haven't left the ship, and they know I'm supposed to meet them for breakfast." He checked his watch—thank God for the glow-in-the-dark dial on the old thing. "In fifteen minutes."

"When he can't find you, Scott will think you ditched him." He sounded so smug.

Gary held his head, the pain slipping away. God, the man was dumb. "Are you going to hold me in here for the rest of the cruise? What about Phillip?"

Frank began to laugh. "I lifted his sea pass so he can't get back in."

"All he has to do is get another one, and they'll deactivate that one." The laughing stopped. Gary started to wonder what Frank would do when he was truly backed into a corner. "Frank, you really haven't done anything to hurt me. Just open the door and let me go."

"No." He sounded like a kid who'd had his toys taken away. "Scott has to pay somehow and since he likes you, I'm going to take you away."

Jesus, the guy was really messed up. Gary began feeling around for anything he could use as a weapon. Running his hand over the shelf, his fingers encountered one of Phillip's belts with a big heavy buckle. He wasn't sure how he could use it, but having it in his hands made him feel less vulnerable. "Frank, you're not going to take me anywhere, and if you keep this up, when they find me, the only person who'll be going anywhere is you. To prison."

"No, I won't. At sea, the captain is law."

"We're not at sea; we're docked in St. Croix, a U.S. territory." There was no response. "Look, Frank, I know you hate Scott for what you think he did to your sister, but he didn't do anything to her."

"He killed her," Frank said softly as his voice began to break.

"No, he didn't. He was proven innocent of ever hurting her." Gary realized this wasn't going to get him anywhere so he tried another tack. "I know you need someone to blame for her death, and it's easy to blame Scott, but sometimes no one is to blame. Sometimes bad things happen." Gary listened for a reaction and thought he heard a soft whimper of some kind. "Let go of the hate, and move on with your life."

"I can't!" The door began to vibrate, and Gary wasn't sure what was going on, then the movement stopped.

Gary continued, keeping his voice level and calm. "Yes, you can. Do you think your sister would want you throwing your life away like this? Or would she want you to be happy?" Gary kept listening, but his words were met with silence.

A knock on the outside door made Gary jump. "I'm in here! Get help!" Gary yelled through the door. "See, Frank, it was that easy. These walls are paper thin and don't keep out any sound whatsoever. It's time you let me out."

Nothing. No movement or sound. Gary pushed on the closet door lightly, and it opened. Pushing slowly, the door opened, revealing only a dark room. Gary banged the door open hard, but it just met the stops and bounced back. Then Gary heard a card slide in the lock and pulled open the door to a surprised steward standing with Scott and Sam right behind him.

"Are you okay?" Scott pushed past the others and rushed inside, hugging Gary to him. "We saw Frank hurrying down the hall."

"I'm fine," Gary mumbled against Scott's chest, his head plastered against the wall of flesh. He managed to pull away slightly and looked at the open-mouthed steward. "Thank you so much." Without saying a thing, the man moved away and out of sight.

"What happened?" Sam closed the door, and Scott sat on the bed, pulling Gary down next to him.

Gary looked up at the folded arms of the stern policeman. "I'm fine, Sam, you can relax." Gary told them what Frank had done, and what he'd said.

"I must have gotten to him because he just left." Gary did his best to make light of the incident. "I swear I heard him crying at one point."

"I'll kill him!"

Gary placed a hand on Scott's arm, stilling the big man with a touch. "No. He's confused as it is, and escalating is just going to make things worse. He's hurting and wants someone to blame, but I think that's getting old, even for him. Just let him be. I doubt we'll have any more issues with him."

"How do you know? He's already escalated things." Sam walked to the table and picked up the phone.

"Don't, Sam. He's grieving for someone he's lost and doesn't know where to turn. Hate's easy. It's forgiving and moving on that's hard. Besides, he really didn't hurt me." Gary looked at Scott. "I want to enjoy what time we've got left before you go back to Pennsylvania, and I go back to Milwaukee, okay?"

Scott nodded, and Gary looked over at Sam, pleading with his eyes.

"Okay," Sam put the phone down. "But I don't want either of you to be alone. Either stay together or make sure someone else is with you." Sam's eyes looked stern.

Gary saluted. "Yes sir, officer."

Sam walked toward the door. "Smart-ass kids."

Gary began to laugh. "Thanks, Sam. We'll see you upstairs in a few minutes."

The door closed, and Scott looked at him, his body rigid, eyes toward the floor, acting like he was waiting for something. Gary stared at him, wondering what was wrong.

"Aren't you mad at me?" Scott asked.

"No. Why would I be mad at you?"

Scott's eyes lifted from the floor. "It's because of me that Frank shoved you in the closet."

Gary huffed softly. "I'm not mad at you, and it's not your fault." Gary took Scott's hand. "You have to stop blaming yourself for other people's actions." He kissed Scott's knuckles. "You're the one who helped rescue me, remember?" Scott nodded but didn't look convinced. "I'm fine." He patted Scott's knee. "Now let's get some breakfast, I'm starved. Being shut in the closet for a whole ten minutes really works up an appetite."

Gary smiled and actually saw Scott try to suppress one of his own. Then he tickled Scott's side, and the big man squirmed away. "Man, I didn't know you were ticklish." Gary went at him, tickling him without mercy until Scott was rolling with laughter and squirming any way he could to get out of the reach of Gary's fingers.

"Gary." Scott was curled into a ball on the bed, trying to defend all his ticklish spots, and Gary stepped back so Scott could catch his breath, both of them laughing.

"Let's go eat."

Scott uncurled himself slowly and stood up, keeping his distance from Gary as he breathed like he'd run a marathon. "Aren't you ticklish?" Gary could see the gleam in Scott's eye.

"Nope." Gary wiggled his fingers in Scott's direction, and Scott made a dash for the door. Gary followed, putting his hands down. "Come on, let's eat."

They found the guys upstairs and joined them at the table. Sam had obviously already filled everyone in on the morning's excitement, and after a few questions, they settled down to eat before getting ready to leave the ship.

St. Croix was pretty, but there wasn't much on the side of the island where the ship docked, so they wandered around and did some final shopping. Finding a small beach, they waded in the water and collected small shells and bits of glass. It didn't really matter what they did. Gary felt free, and they could just have fun. He was sure Frank wouldn't bother them anymore. Now, if he could just figure out how to keep from having to say good-bye to Scott tomorrow, life would be perfect. "What are you going to do with those?" Scott asked as Gary showed him the small, rounded, pebble-like pieces.

"I'm going to give them to a designer client of mine. He'll find something interesting to do with them."

Scott's finger moved the pieces around in Gary's hand. "Okay, but what are they?"

"It's sea glass." Gary held one to the light. "It's pieces of broken bottles and stuff that have been tumbled by the waves. They look almost jewellike because the sea polishes them." Gary knew Fabrizio would get a kick out of them.

Scott picked up one and peered through it. "Cool." He set the piece back in Gary's hand like it was a fine gem, and then began looking for his own bits. It quickly became a game to see who could find the most interesting piece in the most unusual color.

They headed back to the ship at lunch time, their treasures stowed in their bags. Most of the other guys had decided to take a shuttle to the other side of the island, so Gary and Scott enjoyed the buffet alone. Gary found himself watching every move Scott made, and he kept touching the man. They only had today and tonight, and he was determined to get as many touches and, when they were alone, kisses as he could.

After lunch, they spent the afternoon together, swimming, lounging, and soaking, listening to the live music. They were never far from each other, and, in private moments, they'd touch or brush against each other. Gary was conscious of every hour that passed, and he could tell Scott was too. They went rock climbing together, racing to the top, and Scott won. They played mini golf, laughing their asses off because the only clubs available were for kids, so they played all hunched over. This time, Gary won. They grabbed basketballs and shot baskets, but neither won since they were both terrible at it. But they laughed and joked away the afternoon at whatever they were doing, and they talked. Not superficial things— they really talked. It seemed to Gary as though nothing was off limits, and it felt good to be free and open with someone about everything. Then the sun began to set. They both watched it sinking into the sea, the end of a great day and the beginning of the end of their vacation and time together.

Gary felt Scott's hand on top of his as he gripped the rail, and Gary turned to look at Scott. "I need to tell you something," Gary whispered, as he looked deep in Scott's eyes.

Scott lightly placed his finger over Gary's lips. "Don't, please." Scott shook his head, and Gary felt his heart wrench, thinking Scott didn't feel the same way he did. "Don't say it. Once the words are out, you can't take them back, and we go home tomorrow." Gary stared out at the glistening water, feeling his eyes begin to fill. He felt Scott's arm slide around his shoulders, pulling him against his side. "I know, Gary, me too."

They stood for a long time, watching the sun dip below the waves as darkness descended over the water. Neither of them moved or spoke. Gary knew if he tried, the words would get caught in his throat anyway, so he stayed where he was, holding on to Scott. As darkness took over and the ship began to move, Scott let his arm fall. Taking Gary's hand, he led him back inside. Scott didn't say anything—he just led Gary by the hand. People looked twice, and Gary saw a few shake their heads, but Scott would glare at them, and they'd back down from whatever they were going to say.

Gary wanted to ask what Scott was doing but didn't. He just followed Scott into the elevator and then down the passageway to Scott's cabin. Once inside, Gary was taken into strong arms, and Scott kissed him, hard, like he was staking a claim, and Gary felt himself melt into the touch, moaning softly.

There was a sharp knock on the door, and Scott pulled away. Gary huffed softly and sat on the edge of the bed as Scott opened the door. "Are you coming to dinner?" He recognized Dan's voice.

"We'll see you there," Gary heard Scott reply, and then the door closed, and Scott was back with him, pushing him down onto the bed, kissing him hard enough to make his head spin.

"Scott," Gary begged softly as he slipped his hand under Scott's shirt.

In response, Scott held his hand and moved it away. "Later. Right now I just want to be with you. We have all night for that." Gary felt Scott's arms wind around his neck and pull their lips close. Gary melted at the feel of those lips, and as he opened his mouth, Scott's tongue accepted his silent invitation and the flavors, Scott's and his, combined on his tongue, his senses going into overdrive. Scott's tongue slipped back, tracing the ridge of his lips, and then Scott sucked his lower lip, tugging erotically.

Gary's pleasure and contentment resounded in his chest like he was purring, and Scott smiled against his lips and kept on kissing him. There was no hurry, no rush, and Gary felt like he was being savored, committed to memory, which was exactly what he was doing with every touch, sound, and taste of Scott.

Gary ran his hands over Scott's back to ground himself as his head began to spin. His body thrummed, the slightest touch sending shivers through him. He had no idea how long they kissed— minutes, hours—it didn't matter. The time slipped by quickly, and all too soon, Scott was pulling away. "I think we're going to be late for dinner."

Gary nodded slowly, his hand going to his swollen, happy lips. He hadn't ever necked like that, and he couldn't believe how arousing and sexy it felt just to kiss. "I need to change." Gary got up from the bed, and his head swam for a minute. Slowly, steadying himself, he made his way to the door. Turning back, he saw the self-satisfied smile on Scott's face before he left the cabin.

Feeling a little drunk, he found himself tottering down the passages and stairs to his own cabin.

Phillip glanced up as he entered. "Someone's been thoroughly kissed." He began to laugh.

"Looks like both of us have seen a little action this afternoon." Gary returned Phillip's laugh. "I take it your cowboy's a good kisser." Phillip actually demurred, and Gary laughed harder. "Now that's something I thought I'd never see: a bashful Phillip." A pillow sailed by his head, and Gary picked it up, tossing it back. "What are you going to do tomorrow?" Gary asked as he sat on the bed.

"I think the more important question is what are *you* going to do tomorrow?" Phillip sat next to him, massaging his shoulders. "You really like him, don't you?" Gary nodded slowly, afraid to say anything. "I know. I like Dakota, too, but it's time to go home."

Gary swallowed. "You keep telling yourself that, and maybe you'll start to believe it." Gary looked at Phillip and saw his own feelings reflected in his friend's eyes. They both were going to have a hard time of it tomorrow.

Phillip was the first to shake off the blues. "Come on, the cruise isn't over yet, and we both have sexy men to get ready for." Phillip was right, so Gary shook off his own gloomy feelings and began to change for dinner. "Besides good-bye sex is almost as hot as make-up sex." Phillip tried to dodge the pillow Gary threw, but he moved too late.

Chapter 14

DINNER was great, with everyone laughing and talking. Lonnie was in what Dan described as rare form. The man told stories all through dinner, stories that should never be told in polite company—hell, stories that should never be told outside a locker room—but he was entertaining. Gary had listened, but his thoughts were elsewhere. He kept looking over at Scott, trying to figure out how he could get away from this sense of impending loss. He knew the cruise would end and that they'd go their separate ways, but that didn't mean he had to be happy about it.

After finishing dinner and giving his waiters their tip envelopes, Gary got up from the table and followed his dining companions out. "Can we go for a walk?"

"Sure, but don't you need to pack?"

"I did that before dinner, so I'm all yours."

Scott smiled and took his hand, leading him to the elevators. Together they rode up to the pool deck and stepped out into the humid night air. The deck was largely deserted, and they strolled slowly as the ship pitched slightly from side to side. "I'm not ready to go home."

"I'm not, either. It seems like we just boarded yesterday, and tomorrow we go home." Gary sighed loudly. "I never expected to meet someone, and then when I do, he lives in another part of the country." Life just wasn't very fucking fair. There had to be a way; he just hadn't thought of it yet.

"Are you sorry?" There was a touch of fear in Scott's voice.

"Not for a minute." Gary might feel bad that he had to go home, but he would never regret the time he had with Scott, even if it was going to end. "This has been the best week of my life."

"Really?" Scott asked as they continued walking around the deck, seeing a few people soaking in the hot tubs.

"Yes, and I wouldn't trade it for anything." Even the heartache he knew was coming would be worth the time he'd had with Scott. Gary turned and saw Scott's warm smile as they continued their walk around the ship. Scott led them inside and to the stairs. They both picked up their pace as they made their way into the ship and to Scott's door.

Once inside the cabin, Gary found himself pressed against the door with Scott's lips on his. He felt a pair of warm hands slip beneath his shirt and fingers began plucking his nipples. Gary whimpered softly and felt his knees begin to shake. "Scott!" Any further words were cut off by insistent lips.

"I'll take care of you, Gary," Scott murmured against Gary's lips, as his hands got busy, and Gary felt fingers at his nipples again, worrying them until he could barely see straight. "I love how sensitive you are. How you respond to my touch." Scott's lips traveled to Gary's ear. "Love how you make me feel."

Gary tried to respond, but his breath was stolen again by Scott's wandering hands and he gave up, resting his head back against the door and letting Scott have his erotic way with him.

Scott began opening his shirt, parting the fabric and then swirling his tongue around one nipple. Gary kept himself plastered against the door. It was the only way he could remain standing as his knees and legs began to shake in earnest. "My legs are giving out." Gary felt Scott's arms slip behind him, and he was lifted off the floor and carried to the bed. He bounced as Scott set him on the mattress, and he looked up into those huge warm eyes surrounded by cascades of long, black hair.

"You should probably get naked."

Gary swallowed and vibrated with excitement at the passion that shone in Scott's eyes. Gary moved quickly, shedding his clothes and lying back on the bed, feeling really naughty being naked when Scott was still fully clothed. But all he could feel at the moment were Scott's eyes on him, taking him in from head to toe. Then, slowly, Scott began to undress. The shirt slipped off Scott's shoulders, shoes thunked on the floor, and pants slid down powerful legs, puddling on the carpet.

Gary's mouth began to water as Scott stepped closer, his heavy erection pointing the way. Gary reached toward him, but Scott gently placed his arms on the bed, and his hands began stroking Gary's skin. Every touch made Gary want more.

"Close your eyes, Gary." The hands kept stroking, and Gary slowly lowered his eyelids. "Just feel."

Gary's skin was going wild, every nerve firing as Scott touched him. He felt the bed shift as Scott joined him, and he inhaled deeply as he felt warm lips stroke along his cock. Clamping his eyes closed, he held his breath as Scott's lips slid down his length, taking him deep and hot before sliding back. "Few people have ever believed in me the way you have."

Gary's breath flew from him as Scott took him to the root, sucking hard, releasing his hold, and then sucking again. Gary's legs throbbed on the bedding, and he kept his eyes closed, letting himself feel everything Scott was doing to him, committing every touch to memory. Scott pushed every button he had, and Gary couldn't last. As much as he wanted to, he was way too excited, and he came in a rush that left him gasping and seeing stars.

When he'd caught his breath, Gary felt Scott's lips against his, and then he felt Scott's weight. Gary wound his legs around Scott's waist, opening himself to his lover for what he was afraid would be the last time. Fingers teased his skin, skimming over his opening. "Scott, want you so much."

A wrapper tore, Scott shifted and then returned, and Gary felt himself being filled in the most exquisite way possible. Gary closed his eyes and committed everything to memory: the feel of Scott's skin, the way he stretched him, the taste of his lips, the silky softness of his hair as it fell forward, rubbing against Gary's face. He wanted to remember it all—the firmness of Scott's thrusts, the small sounds he made, the way he touched him, and the way he could make him feel so excited he was ready to come for the second time in ten minutes.

Scott began panting, and his thrusts became ragged. Gary could hold back no longer as Scott's hand glided along his length, and he gasped into Scott's kiss and came as Scott stilled, throbbing deep inside him.

All remained motionless, as if the very ship were holding its breath. Scott didn't move and Gary looked up at him, eyes questioning.

"I don't want to move and break this connection." Scott's body was taut, muscles rippling with strain.

Gary ran his hands along Scott's chest. He didn't want the connection broken, either, so neither of them moved until their bodies took over and separated of their own accord.

Scott moved slowly, getting off the bed and returning with a warm cloth. Gary was lovingly and carefully cleaned up, and then Scott joined him in bed. The lights darkened, the room stilled, and Gary was held tight as lips lightly brushed over his. "What are we going to do?" The words were so soft they barely reached Gary's ears.

"I wish I knew. We've only known each other for less than a week, but I'm going to feel a little lost without you." Gary rolled onto his side, his face inches from Scott's. "Why isn't life fair? I meet someone, someone…." Gary stopped, trying to find the right words, but gave up and spoke from his heart. "Someone I could spend the rest of my life with, someone who likes me, and he lives in another part of the country." Gary buried his face against Scott's chest because he could feel tears trying to come, and he didn't want that. He didn't want one of Scott's last memories of the trip to be of him crying like a baby. "I know life isn't fair," he mumbled against Scott's chest. *But damn it, they both deserved a break.*

"I know." Scott's hands soothed along Gary's back. "I know. But it doesn't work that way."

Gary tried to imagine what Scott was thinking. His life, more than most, truly demonstrated that life wasn't fair. But they couldn't *make* it fair, and they couldn't magically wish things were better. With a deep sigh, he held on to Scott and breathed in his scent, memorizing the feel of his skin. Gary fell asleep trying to hold on to every memory he could.

"Get off him! Don't hurt him!"

Gary woke with a start, the covers pulling away from him as Scott sat up in bed, shouting.

"Scott, you're here, you're safe." Gary rubbed his arm gently and turned on a light. "It's okay. No one is hurting anyone." He saw Scott's eyes open and look around frantically. "You're okay." Gary ran his hands across Scott's back, trying to soothe him.

"I'm sorry." Scott let his body recline back on the mattress. "I was there, in prison again."

"I know. You did the same thing earlier in the week. It's okay. I'm here." Gary continued stroking Scott's skin to calm him. "Do you have these dreams often?" He might have asked that question before, he couldn't remember, but he hoped to get Scott talking a little before trying to go back to sleep.

Scott nodded. "They used to happen every night, but…." Scott stopped and turned toward him. "I haven't had one in days, not since the first night we slept together." Gary turned off the light, and they got comfortable again. "I guess that means there's hope that they'll go away."

To Gary it meant that they should stay together, but he couldn't say that. "I think so." Gary snuggled close and listened for a while as Scott's breathing evened out. Eventually Gary drifted off as well, but almost as if Scott's bad dreams were catching, Gary's were restless and disturbing.

The alarm woke them early. Scott turned it off, but Gary didn't move. He didn't want to get up. That was the last step before he had to say good-bye. He held Scott close, tears threatening again, but he willed them back. He could cry later if he had to, but for now, he wasn't going to mourn a loss that hadn't happened yet. Gary held Scott tight, even as he tried to get out of bed.

"We have to get up." Scott's voice sounded raspy and as thick with emotion as Gary knew his would be. Admitting to himself that he couldn't put off the inevitable, he got up as well and began getting dressed. "Are you all set?"

Gary nodded and looked at the clock. "Phillip and I are supposed to disembark in an hour."

"I've got almost three." Scott began dressing as well. "I'll finish up here and meet you for breakfast in fifteen minutes."

"Okay." Gary finished dressing and gave Scott a kiss before leaving.

Phillip was already up and dressed, getting his things together. "We're supposed to wait in the theater to disembark."

Gary rushed around, getting cleaned up and packing the last of his things. "I'm supposed to meet Scott for breakfast in a few minutes."

"Good. I'm meeting Dakota. I'll see you back here in half an hour and we'll head down." Phillip didn't look very happy to be leaving, either. "It'll be fine, Gary. We'll both be fine."

"I know." Gary finished his packing and put the bag on the bed next to Phillip's. Their suitcases had already been taken the night before, and all they had to take were their carry-on bags. They left the room together and made their way through the crowded stairwells to the even more crowded buffet. Gary saw Scott right away. He wasn't really hungry, but he got a little to eat and joined him. They ate in near silence. Gary couldn't think of anything to say that would make either of them feel better, and Scott didn't seem to be in a real talkative mood, either.

"Gary, will you call me when you get home?" Scott handed him a piece of paper with a phone number and e-mail address on it.

"Of course." Gary reached into his pocket and pulled out one of his business cards with all of his contact information on it. "I promise I'll call." Gary's voice broke. "Damn it, I promised myself I wasn't going to do this." Gary picked up his napkin, using it to shield his face as he wiped his eyes.

He felt Scott's hand stroke his and looked up to see Scott standing next to him. "Let's go."

Gary followed Scott out of the dining room and into a small, empty side room where Gary put his arms around Scott's waist and buried his head against his chest. He couldn't control his tears any longer and let them come. He didn't want to leave Scott. He wanted to be together, but that was something that wasn't possible. Gary knew they'd only met less than a week earlier, but the heart wants what it wants, and Gary knew his heart wanted Scott. "I'm sorry." Gary wiped his eyes and tried to pull back, but Scott held him close.

"Don't be." Gary looked up and saw a tear run down Scott's stubbled cheek.

"Will you meet me after we disembark?"

Scott shook his head. "We should say good-bye and not prolong things." Gary knew Scott was right, but he didn't want to let go. Gary felt a finger under his chin, lifting it up. "I'm not good with words, but I'm going to miss you so much. You saw me as good when I didn't see it myself." Gary felt a lump in his throat. "You're a handsome man, Gary, both outside and inside." As Scott leaned down and kissed him, Gary tried to hold himself together. There were so many things he wanted to say, but his voice just wouldn't work. So he returned Scott's kiss and stepped back. "You need to go, or you'll miss your time."

Gary clamped his eyes shut and willed himself not to bawl like a baby as he managed to say good-bye and then left the room, the glass doors hissing behind him as they slid closed. His eyes were so full, he could barely see as he made his way down to his cabin. To his relief, Phillip wasn't there yet. Gary went into the bathroom and dried his eyes with a tissue, trying not to look at his puffy face in the mirror. Phillip came in as Gary finished, and they got their things and left the cabin for the final time. Neither of them spoke much, and for that Gary was grateful.

In the theater, they sat with all the other people and waited for their group to be called before gathering their things for the last time and making their way to the exit doors. They scanned their sea passes one final time and found themselves outside, walking down the same gangway they had used when they'd entered.

In the port building, Gary found his luggage, and, along with Phillip, made his way through Customs and then out to the sidewalk. The other guys had an earlier departure time, but were waiting in a group for him and Phillip. "We were discussing going to Old San Juan before heading to the airport. What do you guys think?" Mark asked as they approached.

"Whatever you'd like to do."

They found a taxi that agreed to take them to the airport with a stop in Old San Juan so they wouldn't have to carry all their bags, and they all loaded into the van. As they pulled away, Gary looked out the window, gazing up at the white hull of the massive ship. Scott was on there somewhere.

"You okay, Gary?" Tyler asked from the seat next to him.

"I'm okay." God, he so wasn't. He was about two seconds from completely falling apart, and he didn't want to do that in front of everyone.

"You know it's okay to miss him and talk about him. We understand."

"Thanks, but I can't, not yet." The emotions were way too close to the surface. Gary felt Tyler pat him on the shoulder. Conversation in the van picked up as everyone talked about the trip and what they liked best. Gary half-listened and stared out the window.

In Old San Juan, he wandered around with Mark and Tyler, going where they wanted and paying little attention to the stores or the scenery. His heart just wasn't in it. After doing some final shopping and looking around, they got back in the van and rode to the airport. Their flight to Chicago was on time and boarded not long after they arrived.

Settling in his seat, Gary stared out the window, watching people load luggage and close doors. Then the plane moved back from the gate and taxied to the runway for takeoff. The engines revved, he was pressed back in his seat, and they raced down the runway. Gary sat uncaring, unaware of the activity around him.

As the plane gained height, they flew over the harbor, and Gary saw the ship below, looking small. Before he could stop himself, he'd raised his hand and waved good-bye. Scott was gone, and Gary doubted he'd ever see him again. He wiped a tear as it fell down his cheek, and continued staring out the window until the clouds and distance obscured the view.

When the seatbelt sign turned off, Gary unhooked his and made his way to the bathrooms, locking the cubicle door behind him. Inside the small room, he pulled a tissue from the dispenser and finally let himself mourn the loss.

Chapter 15

"GARY," Fabrizio called as he entered his shop. "You're back! Did you have fun?" The man hurried over, crushing Gary in a hug. "I hope you brought pictures."

"I did." Gary smiled as the big queen released him after a gentle pat on the butt.

"Good, let's go over things, and we can go to lunch." Fabrizio showed Gary everything he was working on and what he had in mind for it. Then he took Gary into the office, where an award sat on the desk. Fabrizio picked it up and handed it to Gary. "Our display won the judges choice award at the design show," he gushed. "Your fabrics were all the rage. I've got more business than I know what to do with." Fabrizio continued his gushing as he gazed at the award before setting it gingerly back on the desk and leading Gary to his workroom, where they discussed Fabrizio's upcoming projects and what fabrics he was going to need. Since Gary's initial visit, Fabrizio had become one of his best customers. Once everything had been selected, Fabrizio called in his troops and gave them their instructions. "Let's eat. I'm *starved.*" Gary almost laughed at the designer's flamboyance, but stopped himself.

Gary carried his laptop as they walked down the street to a small, quiet bistro. The waiter took their orders, and then Gary set up the laptop.

"This is beautiful. Where is that?"

"Barbados… we were on a catamaran." Gary smiled as he remembered snorkeling with sea turtles and getting to know Scott.

"Who's that delicious man with his arm around you?" Fabrizio asked as he fanned himself. "If I were a little younger...," he lamented.

"His name's Scott." Gary sighed as the picture changed. Looking at the pictures brought back the memories but also the sadness that he'd had to leave Scott behind. The pictures continued, with Fabrizio asking a few questions, and Gary narrating where each one was taken.

"There's that lovely man again."

"That one's on St. Croix. We had some people take our picture for us." Gary loved that photograph. They were wearing bathing suits, Scott's arm around his waist, pulling them close together, both grinning at the camera. The picture changed, and in this one Scott was looking at him.

Gary smiled, truly smiled, when he saw the harmless gleam in Fabrizio's eye. "So, when do I get to meet him?" The lecherous old queen.

Gary felt his smile fade. "He lives in Pennsylvania."

They came to the end of the pictures, and their food arrived, the waiter putting down the plates and then leaving them alone. "Gary, Gary, Gary." Fabrizio shook his head and tsk'd before taking his first bite and swallowing. "That man loves you. And let me guess, you love him too."

Gary swallowed. "It's complicated."

Fabrizio kept eating and shaking his head. "Let me tell you something, baby boy, love is not to be trifled with, and that man loves you. He may not have said it, but the way he looked at you in that picture, it's so obvious." Fabrizio began eating again. "How often do you talk to him?"

"Almost every day." Since he'd gotten back two weeks earlier, those calls were usually the highlight of Gary's day. They had exchanged e-mails as well, and the first thing Gary did whenever he got up or got home was check to see if there was a note from Scott.

"Are you in love with him?" Fabrizio asked.

Gary nodded and set his lunch aside, suddenly not very hungry.

"Did you tell him?"

"No, not in so many words." He almost explained that he'd tried, but those details weren't for anyone but himself and Scott.

"But you *do* love him." Fabrizio didn't wait for Gary's response as he continued eating. "Then what are you going to do about it?"

"What can I do about it? He's in Harrisburg, and I'm in Milwaukee. He has his life, and I have mine," Gary said, his voice rising. He saw people turn to look at him and, embarrassed, he lowered his voice. "There's nothing I can do about it but get over it and move on."

"But you're not, Gary. You're talking to him every night, e-mailing him, and if I'm not mistaken, looking forward to every note and every phone call. If you truly wanted to get over him, you would have nothing more to do with him." Fabrizio smiled indulgently as he continued. "Listen to an old prissy queen who's been around the block a few times. You don't want to give up those calls to Scott because they're the one link you have to the man you love, and that's good. But you need to do something. Either end it, and let him go, so you can go on, too, or do something about it."

"What should I do?"

Fabrizio smiled. "Have you asked him about the possibility of moving here?"

Gary shook his head. "I can't ask him to do that. We knew each other for a week. I can't expect him to pick up everything and move here, any more than I could move there. It just isn't practical."

"Well, why the hell not? Maybe he's just waiting to be asked." Fabrizio raised his eyebrows expectantly, smiled indulgently, and finished his lunch. Their conversation thankfully shifted to business, and Gary found his appetite returning and finished his own lunch.

After they were done, Gary followed Fabrizio back to the shop, where he checked on all his orders, got him delivery times, and said good-bye before returning to his car to head to Tyler's. He knew Fabrizio was right, but he wasn't sure what to do about it. He had to work and couldn't take time off. Getting in the car, he closed the door and started the engine, pulling out of his parking space. He had to do something.

After driving through busy traffic, he got to the store and managed to find a parking space. The store looked great, as usual, and when he entered, he found Tyler behind his desk working at the computer. Tyler looked up as the bell on the door jingled.

"Hey, Gary, you getting back to normal?"

"Yeah, I just stopped by to see if you needed anything."

Tyler smiled and got up. "No. Everything's great, but stop in next week. I've got some pieces arriving that I'll need fabric to finish." Gary made a note in his planner and looked up, seeing Tyler's smile. "What did you really stop for?"

"I can't fool you, can I?"

"Nope. You've been quiet, even for you, and I know you're missing Scott."

"Yeah. I want to see him again, be with him again, but I can't, and I don't know how to get over it." Gary knew he was whining a little, but Tyler was the one person he knew who would understand. He was as close to a best friend as Gary had ever had. "Fabrizio thinks I should make some sort of move, that I shouldn't let love get away. But I don't know what to do. This is real life, not a soap opera, and sometimes these things don't work out."

Tyler's expression darkened. "Then how come you're talking to him every day and e-mailing him constantly? You can't fool me, and you know it. I saw how you looked at each other, and how you lit up whenever you saw him. You need to admit to yourself that you love him and figure out what you want to do."

"Fabrizio said that too."

Tyler grinned. "He may be the biggest queen either of us will ever know, but the man knows about love. He held a torch for one man for ten years. He knows about taking a chance on love."

"What happened?" Gary was intrigued.

"You'll have to ask him yourself." A customer came into the store, and Tyler excused himself, returning a while later. "By the way, Mark and I decided to have everyone over for an after-cruise get-together this Saturday. Can you come?"

"Sure, I'd love to." Gary got up to leave.

"Good." Tyler smiled and went back to his customer, and Gary left the store, heading home for the day. The gods of traffic were with him, and he was able to find a parking space right outside his building.

Gary unlocked his door and walked into the dark apartment. Turning on the lights, he wandered through the rooms on his way to his bedroom to take a shower. Flipping on the light, he stripped off his clothes, throwing them in the hamper. As he stepped into the bathroom, his phone rang. Gary grabbed it from near the bed.

"Hi, Gary."

He couldn't help smiling. "Scott."

"Did you just get home?"

"Yeah." Gary sat on the edge of the bed. "I was just about to get cleaned up."

The line was silent. "Are you naked?" Scott's voice got deeper, and Gary felt himself shiver in the warm room.

"Yeah." Gary's breath caught.

"I bet you look really hot lying back on your bed." Scott's voice was so seductive, so rich, that Gary went with it, stretching out on the bed, his erection already throbbing. "Are you on the bed?"

Gary swallowed hard. "Uh-huh."

"Don't touch yourself… yet." Gary heard rustling on the line, and he knew Scott was shucking his clothes as well. He could see the man's skin, his long hair, those powerful muscles, and that thick, full cock. "There, I'm on my bed, naked, thinking of you."

Gary moaned a little.

"Touch yourself, Gary, run your hands over your chest."

Gary did, closing his eyes, pretending it was Scott.

"Run your hand over your nipples, pluck 'em. Feel those little points."

Gary was instantly back on the ship with Scott. "I can feel you, almost see you."

"That's it, baby, stroke yourself. I'm thinking of you. I can feel your hand on me, your lips kissing me."

Gary swallowed hard, completely lost in the fantasy, and it felt so good. Spreading his legs wide, he stroked himself, Scott's voice driving him higher.

"You're so lovely, all laid out on the bed for me to touch and taste. Do you want me to taste you Gary... take you all the way... run my tongue down your length?"

"Yes, Scott, yes!" Gary was nearly flying, his breathing coming in shallow gasps. "I feel you, Scott, feel you inside me. I want that, Scott, want that so bad, want you." Gasping for air Gary kept stroking, his entire body shaking. Eyes clamped shut, he was almost there.

"Gonna fill you, make us one, make you mine."

That was it. Gary stroked himself hard, and he came. Eyes clamped shut, body clenched, breath ragged, he gasped into the phone, "Scott," as he spilled onto his stomach, crying out softly and whimpering.

As he came back into himself, he heard Scott panting softly on the other end of the line, a cry, and then Gary heard his lover's own heavy breathing. In his mind's eye, he could see Scott's strong body, long hair disheveled on the pillow, as he came. He looked so beautiful.

The line went quiet, and Gary slowly opened his eyes, the fantasy fading as he looked at his own bedroom. Turning his head, he actually checked for Scott, but he wasn't there, and the phone was still tucked to his ear. His first reaction was disappointment as he heard Scott's voice again. For a second he'd been so caught up in the fantasy that he'd almost fooled himself that Scott was with him.

"I miss you, Gary." The soft words broke him out of his thoughts.

"I miss you too." Gary suddenly felt cold and pulled the duvet over himself as the longing and loneliness began to take over. "I wish you were here with me."

"I know." Gary barely heard Scott's voice. "How was work today?" Whenever Gary tried to talk about them getting together somehow, Scott changed the subject, and Gary knew what it meant. He had to stop this and move on, but the sound of Scott's voice pulled him in like it did every time they talked, and Gary found himself telling Scott all about his day and asking Scott about his.

Neither of them understood what was truly happening in each other's lives. Scott didn't know about the fabric business, and Gary found himself skipping over things, and he knew Scott was doing the same. Maybe this was how it happened. Maybe they'd just drift apart a little at a time. "Scott, do you think we could talk?"

"Sure, Gary." He seemed wary.

"I talked to my supervisor about the possibility of an open position in your area of the country."

"You did? You'd do that? Move here to be with me?" He seemed taken aback. "You'd give up your life and friends there to take a chance on me? Gary, you barely know me."

"I know enough." Gary stopped pushing. Maybe this wasn't what Scott wanted. "If you don't want to be together, just tell me, and I'll stop bothering you." He was feeling hurt and quite embarrassed. They'd just had phone sex. He was still sticky from it, but it sounded like Scott didn't want him anymore.

"It isn't that. I want to be with you. The time we spent together on the cruise was the happiest I've ever been." The words seemed to tumble out of the phone. "And I look forward to each phone call, each e-mail."

"Then what is it, Scott? What's wrong?" Gary didn't understand where Scott was heading.

"Nothing's wrong. I just don't want you giving up your life for me."

"Then what do you want?"

"I don't know, Gary. I just don't know. Everything seems so complicated." Scott sounded confused.

Gary realized that was the million-dollar question. He knew Scott had been through a lot and so many things in his life were new and changing. "Let me ask you this. You want to be with me, right?"

"Yes, very much."

"And I want to be with you, so we just have to decide if we go there or come here."

"It's not that simple."

"But it is."

"Gary." He sounded frustrated, and Gary felt confused and rejected. He'd actually offered to move to Pennsylvania, and Scott had turned him down.

"I'm sorry, Scott," His emotions were beginning to get the best of him. "I need to finish getting cleaned up."

"Me too." They said their good-byes, and Gary placed the phone in its cradle. He was so confused and hurt and, if he was honest with himself, a little heartbroken. When he'd asked his supervisor about moving, he'd said it was a possibility, and then Gary had heard that the position for the central PA and northern Maryland territory might be open soon. The woman who had it was pregnant and wasn't planning on coming back after she had the baby. It seemed to Gary like the perfect solution, but....

Gary huffed softly to himself and got off the bed, going into the bathroom. "Maybe it's time I faced reality. We had a great time on the cruise, but now we're home, and it's time to go on." He looked at himself in the mirror. The idea was a tough sell. His heart wanted Scott, and if he was honest with himself, so did his head. "Why does everything have to be so complicated?" Turning away from the sink, he started the shower and stepped under the spray, washing away his release. He closed his eyes and a vision of a tall, strong Scott popped into his head, body wet, stepping out of the water and walking across the beach, eyes shining and looking at him. "That's what I want," he murmured to himself.

Gary stepped back out of the spray, his eyes open, staring at the tile. Maybe that was the problem. Maybe what he wanted was just an illusion that had lasted a week but then shattered as soon as they'd come into port. Maybe he couldn't have what he wanted because it wasn't real. Gary turned off the water and stepped out, drying himself. He'd known disappointment in his life, but he couldn't remember ever feeling quite so empty.

Chapter 16

A KNOCK on his door got Gary moving. He answered it and ushered Phillip inside. "You're not ready yet?" Phillip asked as he flopped down on the sofa. "You need to get moving or we'll be late."

"Since when are you Mr. Punctual?" Gary went back into his bedroom, talking to Phillip through the open door as he finished dressing. "What's got you all excited anyway?" Gary pulled on his pants and grabbed his shirt from the bed.

Phillip was quiet for a second, and Gary peeked out of the room to see Phillip chewing his nails. He pulled his finger out of his mouth and then answered. "Nothing in particular." Gary knew he was covering up something. "Tyler just said not to be late."

Gary went back to dressing and began wondering if something was going on. "No way," he whispered to himself. Slipping on his shirt, he tucked it in and finished dressing, then joined Phillip in the living room. Phillip could barely sit still, and Gary knew something was up, but he cut his friend some slack and didn't press it. He got his coat and said, "Let's go before you jump out of your skin."

"I heard from Dakota today." Phillip grinned. So that was it. "Have you heard from Scott?"

Gary knew Phillip's question was innocent, but he felt his good mood evaporate. "Not lately, no." Their e-mails had dried up, and Scott hadn't called him since earlier in the week. "Maybe it's for the best." Each evening he'd been disappointed when Scott didn't call, and he'd almost picked up the phone a number of times, but stopped himself each time. If Scott wasn't interested, he wasn't going to press him, and maybe it was the best thing anyway. He kept telling himself that, but he sure didn't feel it.

"Long-distance relationships are hard. Maybe he needs time to think." Phillip put his arm around Gary's shoulder as they walked to the elevator.

"And maybe he thinks it's over." Gary was sure starting to think it was for him and Scott. "He always called every night, and after I told him about looking into a position where he lives, he just stopped. I don't need a house to fall on me to get the message." The elevator arrived, and they rode down, leaving the building and getting into Phillip's car for the ride to Mark and Tyler's.

The house was lit up like the proverbial Christmas tree even though it wasn't quite Thanksgiving yet, but that didn't seem to bother Mark and Tyler. There were trees lining the walk covered in white lights and angel wreaths on each window. "Looks like Tyler let Mark run wild again."

"Again?" Gary asked as he peered out the window.

"Yeah, every year Tyler swears he's going to put out a sign that says 'Scrooge' and every year Mark ignores him and decorates to the hilt." They parked and walked up the path as the front door opened, and Tyler stepped outside. "Look at all this. It looks like Christmas exploded on our house."

Mark followed behind him, hitting Tyler's shoulder. "You love it, and you know it." The two of them shared a smile and then greeted Gary and Phillip, ushering them into the house. "I won't decorate inside until next week." Mark took their coats. "Everyone is in the family room. Just go on back."

Gary followed Phillip through the house to a large, comfortable room where Sam, Sean, Tom, and Bill, along with Kenny and Bobby, were talking and laughing, a huge flat-screen television dominating one wall. "Everyone sent me their pictures and Mark put them together in a slide show," Tyler said. "So everyone eat, and we'll get started soon. We're just waiting for a few more guests, and they're on their way."

A buffet had been set up on the table, and they helped themselves to the food as the doorbell rang. As he waited his turn, Gary heard Mark's voice greeting the guests, and he turned as Dan and Gene walked in the room. Everyone greeted their friends and introductions were made to Bobby and Kenny. *What were they doing here?* Voices filled with laughter drifted in as Gary stopped filling his plate, hope welling inside. He felt a tap on his shoulder. Turning around, he found himself looking into Scott's big eyes.

Gary stopped moving, stunned, wondering if he could believe his eyes. "Scott, what...?" He looked around and saw everyone looking at them with knowing smiles on their faces. "How? When?' He managed to put his plate down, and then Scott's hands were on his cheeks, and he was being kissed. Gary managed to get his arms around Scott's neck and the rest of the world disappeared as his heart soared. Scott was here. Scott was kissing him.

Whistles and catcalls brought Gary back to the present, and he found himself blushing big time as he pulled away from Scott's lips and turned around to face his friends. "Did you all know about this?" Heads nodded, and smiles turned into huge grins. Even big-mouth Phillip had managed to keep this a secret. Gary returned their smiles as Scott slipped his arm around his waist, pulling him close.

"You two should eat before we get started," Tyler said through his grin, as he sat down with his plate. Gary picked up his plate and handed Scott one to fill, waiting for him to do so before they sat together on the sofa. They ate, grinning and glancing at each other between bites. Gary could hardly believe Scott was here. He had a million questions and tried to ask them but got interrupted. "Mark created a slideshow of our trip." Tyler turned to where Mark was working with his laptop.

"It's all set," Mark said, and Tyler turned on the television. Pictures of the ship flashed on the screen followed by pictures of each couple as they boarded the ship, including a picture of Gary and Phillip smiling crazily at the camera. Pictures of the ship's interior followed, along with various shots of them lying out by the pool. There were pictures of them rock climbing, including ones of Gary and Scott racing to the top. Gary scooted closer to Scott and felt him take his hand.

Pictures of the catamaran snorkeling trip in Barbados
followed. There were shots on the boat, and pictures of snorkeling,
underwater photos of sea turtles and shipwrecks along with a few
shots of Tyler mugging for the camera that brought laughter from
everyone. The trip in pictures continued with the stop in St. Lucia,
kayaking in Antigua, and pictures around the table and in the
restaurant for Tom's birthday.

Gary gawked at a shot of Scott walking out of the surf with
glistening skin, his long hair wet, the tattoo on his shoulder
sparkling with drops of water. "That's an amazing picture of you."
Scott smiled back at him as the picture changed to one of Gary being
carried into the water. He could feel Scott's arms around him, and
he moved closer still, practically climbing onto Scott's lap. These
pictures of Scott were making him horny, and he had to adjust
himself to a more comfortable position.

The trip pictures continued with more of St. Maarten and then
St. Croix. Toward the end of the show, a picture of him and Scott
that had been taken on deck flashed on the screen. Gary stared at the
picture. It was a great one of Scott, but he realized the more
powerful expression in the photograph was his. Gary felt goose
bumps travel down his back as he looked at the picture. Gary saw all
his emotions for Scott laid naked for everyone to see there on the
screen. The way his lips were slightly parted, the way his eyes
gleamed, a small smile—all of it locked on Scott. Gary couldn't
move. He just stared at the picture, then at Scott and then back to the
picture.

Gary let his gaze travel to everyone in the room, checking to
see if he was seeing things, but they were riveted to the picture and
smiling as their gazes slowly switched to him and Scott.

"That is a fucking amazing picture." Bobby broke the silence.
"Who took it?"

Gary noticed Mark shift in his seat, but no one said a thing.
Finally the picture faded and a new one replaced it. But this time it
was one of Scott looking at Gary with an intensity that actually
made Gary shift on his seat. He turned to Scott, but instead of
looking at the screen, Scott was looking at Gary, with the same

intense expression on his face. "Scott." Gary breathed and swallowed hard, not having any idea what to say. They say a picture was worth a thousand words—this one was worth a million. Raw emotional power shone from the screen until it faded to black.

Gary couldn't take his eyes off Scott. He had to know whether that was a fluke or how he really felt. No one in the room moved. It was like a spell had been cast, and they all needed to see what happened. Gary saw Scott move closer. He felt a hand slide to the back of his neck, and then he was being kissed, a kiss he felt deep in his soul. There was no doubt what Scott was feeling—everything poured to him through that kiss. Gary was painfully hard, his body begging for release, wanting Scott to take him right here, right now, and all from a single kiss. Slowly the kiss lessened, and then Scott backed away, his eyes shining. Gary smiled and dove to him, crashing their lips together, devouring Scott until he felt a firm touch on his shoulder bring him back to reality. Gary blushed and sat back in his seat, knowing he was getting redder with each passing second.

Looking around the room, he saw that everyone was staring at them. Finally they began to move and snippets of conversation began. Gary screwed his eyes closed and rested his head on Scott's shoulder to steady himself. He needed a minute to gather his thoughts, with so much racing through his head.

"Tom brought dessert." Tyler's call for sweets had everyone moving around, and Gary breathed a sigh of relief as Scott got up, leaving him alone on the sofa until Tyler sat down next to him.

"You're not mad at me?"

Gary looked at Tyler, confused. "Why? Should I be?"

"You're not angry that I called Scott."

"No, but now that you mention it, why did you do it?"

Tyler smiled and squeezed Gary's knee. "You saw those pictures. When Mark was putting together the show, he showed them to me, and I called Scott and Dan to see if they could come out. I made everyone promise not to tell you in case something happened, and they weren't able to come." Tyler smiled. "Besides I wanted it to be a surprise."

"It was." Gary returned Tyler's smile, looking at Scott getting pieces of cake.

"There's more." Tyler got up as Scott approached, handing Gary a plate and fork. "But I'll let Scott tell you." Tyler went to get himself some cake as Scott sat down.

"What was Tyler referring to?"

Scott shrugged. "We'll talk later," he said, leaning closer, "when we're alone." Scott grinned wickedly and ate another bite of cake as Gary felt a jolt of desire run through him. He held the plate of cake, but he didn't want it. All he wanted to do was run his tongue over Scott's skin, taste the man, feel him, get him naked in his bed. Nothing else mattered and everything narrowed to that one thing.

"Are you almost done?"

Scott finished off the last bite of his cake and nodded. Gary got to his feet, looking for Phillip. He found him getting their coats with a huge grin on his face. "I figured you'd be ready to go."

They said their good-byes to smiles and knowing looks before walking out with Phillip to the car. The drive was quick, and Gary unlocked his door. The door slammed closed, Gary's coat hit the floor, and Scott's arms were around him, holding him, lips kissing him. Gary could hardly believe it: Scott was here, holding him again.

Gary broke away and took Scott by the hand, leading him through the dark apartment toward the bedroom. Turning on a bedside lamp, Gary sat on the edge of the bed and looked up at Scott. He needed to make sure he was real. He reached out to touch him and watched as Scott pulled his shirt over his head, then reached out to Gary and pulled off his shirt before kissing him again. Scott leaned forward, lowering Gary to the bed, their chests rubbing together, heat spreading from one to the other. "I didn't think I'd ever do this again," Gary gasped as Scott released his lips, but further talking was cut off when Scott's lips closed over a nipple, and Gary's breath whooshed away.

Gary's fingers carded through Scott's soft hair as he pushed into the touch, moaning softly, as first one, then the other nipple was sucked and teased. Gary was given a brief reprieve when Scott stood up and slipped off his clothes, then opened Gary's pants, pulling them off along with his shoes and socks. Pulling back the covers, Gary climbed in bed, and Scott joined him, pulling him close. "Gary, I wouldn't let you say it because I was scared, but I love you."

"I love you too." Gary's emotions were so close to the surface, he thought he could feel himself tear up. Then Scott was kissing him again, pressing him into the mattress. Gary felt Scott rubbing against his hip, and he found himself grinding against Scott, returning his kisses. "This is what I wanted, you with me in my bed."

Scott kissed him, and Gary felt him slide down his body. He groaned when Scott's head slipped beneath the covers and cried out when he was engulfed in warm wetness. "Scott." Gary was sucked hard, and he cried out again as Scott worked his hands beneath him, cupping his butt. Gary began bucking, moaning softly as he lost himself in Scott's wetness. Gary's head rolled back and forth on the pillow, his senses overwhelmed as he gasped for breath.

A finger slid over his opening. "Scott, I can't hold it."

He heard a mumble from beneath the covers and felt the finger slide into him, then Gary saw stars, coming in a blinding flash. When he could remember his name again, Scott was lying next to him, a hand petting his skin. "Are you okay?"

Gary smiled, kissing the concerned look off Scott's face. "I'm fine, and you were amazing." They began kissing again, and Gary squirmed his way beneath Scott, opening himself to his lover. A finger slid back inside, and Gary groaned, relishing the sensation of being together. A second finger and then a third finger stretched him as Scott's lips pulled at his, kissing him, and he moaned softly when the lips pulled away and Scott shifted. A package opened and fingers slicked him, then Gary held his breath as Scott entered him, both of them moaning deeply as their bodies joined.

Scott stilled deep inside him. "What do you want, Gary?"

Gary's eyes widened. "You remember the night the people in the next cabin banged on the wall?" Scott nodded, his eyes darkening at the intense memory. "I want that." And he got it. Scott pulled out and drove into him, Gary's body, the bed and, as far as he could tell, the entire building feeling the power. Scott's groans filled the room, and Gary joined in the chorus, both calling out their passion with a complete lack of restraint. His hand was replaced by Scott's, and Gary clung to the blankets as his body was exquisitely and completely pummeled with passion. Gary lost all track of anything other than Scott and the way he was playing his body. This was no gentle lovemaking. This was raw, animalistic passion and longing at its most intense. Gary closed his eyes and rode the crest of passion that Scott was building until it crashed on the shore in a thundering release of pleasure.

The room was quiet except for Scott's panting, as Gary opened his eyes, breath heaving in and out of his body. He could barely remember anything—his release had been that powerful. He saw Scott's arms give out and felt him collapse on top of him, his head near Gary's shoulder, arms tight around his neck. Scott felt good plastered against his skin, held there by their sweat and the remains of their ecstasy. They lay together, holding each other, breathing and whispering things neither could hear but both understood.

Slowly Scott began to move. First it was only his head, shifting to Gary's lips, kissing him as a hand slowly petted his hair. "I don't have the energy to move."

Gary nodded. Kissing suddenly felt like strenuous exercise. "Do you think you can make it to the shower?" he asked, loving the feel of Scott's skin against his. He'd missed this so much. Moving slowly, Scott managed to get to his feet, extending his hand, and together they made it to the bathroom.

Water sluiced over them as hands caressed and re-learned skin and muscle, rekindling the memories of details forgotten during their weeks apart. Lips were put to good use as arms held each other close.

Now clean and toweled dry, they fell into the bed, each still holding the other close. Gary heard Scott's soft snores and smiled at the familiar sound, allowing himself to wonder how it would feel to hear that soft sound every night.

Gary's eyes popped open, his dreamy state vanishing. Scott was going to leave again. He, Dan, and Gene were only visiting, and they were going to go home in a few days. And the warm joy he was feeling was going to be replaced with the same loneliness and longing and wishing he'd become so familiar with the last few weeks. An arm snaked around his chest, pulling him against Scott's warmth, and Gary did his best to try to keep the worries at bay.

Chapter 17

GARY woke in his own bed. Opening his eyes, he was greeted with a pair of bright eyes shining down at him, a smile on Scott's handsome face. "I didn't mean to wake you."

Gary smiled through his yawn and tried to cover his mouth. "You didn't." He hadn't slept well, his mind refusing to let go of the disappointment he knew was coming. "Are you hungry?" Gary squirmed out of the bed and put on his robe.

"Is something wrong? Did I do something?"

Gary tried to muster a convincing smile. "No, not at all." Gary suddenly needed to get away. He had to get where he couldn't see those eyes, that face framed by luxurious hair, and that body that knew exactly how to make his sing. "I just want to make you breakfast." He hoped his cover was convincing. He didn't want to hurt Scott. He just needed a chance to get himself together, or he'd get on his knees and beg Scott to stay. He walked to the kitchen, trying not to rush away, but couldn't stop himself from turning around to see Scott lying on the bed, and it was almost enough to get him to go back to bed.

He busied himself making breakfast. He looked up when he heard footsteps on the floor, and saw Scott walk into the kitchen wearing only his briefs. He tried to hold back the groan, he really did, but it slipped past his lips, weakening his resolve. It crumbled completely when he felt Scott's arms wind around his waist, hands sliding beneath his robe to stroke his stomach.

"When are you going back?" There. The dreaded question had been asked.

"We're leaving Monday morning, early." Two days. All he had with Scott were the next two days. "I know it's not long, but it was all we could get right after the cruise."

Gary turned in Scott's arms, doing his best not to set himself on fire at the stove. "I know." He rested his head against Scott's shoulder. "I just wish you could stay." He knew he wasn't being realistic or even practical, but he gave himself silent kudos for at least saying what he was feeling. Gary looked into Scott's eyes and saw a flicker of something pass across them, and then he saw that same indulgent smile he'd seen on the cruise. "I know we both have our lives."

A soft kiss ghosted across his lips. "I know how you feel. Just give me a little time." Scott unfastened Gary's robe, parting the fabric before bringing their skin into contact. Scott's knee insinuated itself between Gary's legs as their bodies melded together.

"Do you have to work today?" Scott asked.

Gary shook his head.

"Can breakfast wait?"

Gary managed to turn off the burner behind him before he felt the robe slip from his shoulders, puddling on the floor.

Scott lifted him into his arms, carrying him back to the bedroom.

"Going all caveman on me?" Gary asked. His chuckles were cut off as Scott kissed them away. Scott set him on the bed and proceeded to love Gary's worries temporarily out of his head.

The morning glided by in a haze of sated passion. Breakfast became brunch and they finally left the apartment early in the afternoon. Gary had called Tyler, and they agreed to meet at Tyler's Antiques. "We'll bring Scott's suitcase," Tyler said with a knowing chuckle. "We really didn't expect he'd be staying with us, but you left in a slight hurry last night."

They arrived at the store to find Dan and Gene there as well. "We figured you two would surface eventually," Gene said, smiling. "We were going to walk to Sean's wine store. Tyler said it was close. Do you want to go along?"

Gary turned to Scott who shrugged. "You two go ahead. Do you need directions?"

Gene shook his head. "Tyler told us where it was." He and Dan gathered their coats and left the store. Scott began to wander through the display rooms looking at some of the items and occasionally whistling softly when he checked the prices.

"Do people really pay this much?" Scott whispered to Gary as Tyler left to help a customer.

"Yes, they do. I'm told that Tyler's prices are very reasonable, which is why he's so successful," Gary said, looking around. "I think Mark's in his studio. I'm going to go back and say hello."

The door jingled, signaling the customer's exit, and Tyler wandered back over. "Do you think I can borrow Scott for a while?" He turned to Scott. "I could use your help if you don't mind."

Scott nodded.

"I'll be in the studio with Mark," Gary said, making his way through the store to Mark's studio, bright light pouring in its huge windows. Mark was sitting at his easel staring at a mostly blank canvas. He turned as Gary approached.

"Don't mean to interrupt," Gary said.

Mark set down the brush he'd been handling. "You're not. I'm just sitting here staring into space anyway." He got off his stool and pulled a chair up for Gary. "Sometimes things won't come no matter what I do, and I just have to give it a rest." Mark looked around. "Where's Scott?"

"Helping Tyler."

"So were you really surprised last night? No one spilled the beans?"

"Nope, it was a total surprise. Even Phillip managed to keep it a secret."

Mark's smile brightened and then faded as his face became more serious. "Dan told me they're going back on Monday." Gary nodded, his own smile slipping. "I know how you feel, and I have to tell you I didn't totally agree with Tyler on this one. When I showed him those photographs of you and Scott, he convinced me that inviting them was going to be a great surprise." Mark picked up his brush and began fiddling with it nervously. "It's not that I didn't think you'd be happy to see him. I was afraid of how you'd feel when they left again."

"I know how I'm going to feel when they leave." Gary got up and began walking toward the windows. "I'm glad you invited them, and I'm thrilled Scott's here." Gary turned back to Mark. "But it's going to be hard when they leave." *Especially after last night.* He paused, then said, "Scott told me he loves me."

"That's great!" Gary saw Mark's smile reflected in the glass.

"It is. I just wished he loved me enough to stay." Gary heaved a breath and let it out slowly. "Sorry, that wasn't fair to him or you. I just wish that things weren't always so complicated."

Mark began to laugh, and Gary whirled around in complete confusion, furrowing his eyebrows. "I'm sorry." Mark calmed himself, but kept smiling. "You haven't known Tyler long, but I bet he and Scott are talking about more than moving furniture." Mark dropped the brush he was holding back in the holder. "Tyler needs help around the store. He used to have Gladys, but she moved to Florida a few months ago, and Steve took over the deli after his dad died."

"What are you saying? That Tyler's offering Scott a job?" Hope sprang big time.

"Maybe. I don't really know. We haven't talked about it, but I know my Ty." Mark walked to where Gary was standing. "Even if Tyler is offering Scott a job, moving is a big decision. It needs to be Scott's, and he needs to do it for the right reasons."

Gary wanted to ask Mark what he meant, but Scott walked in after a soft knock on the door. The three of them talked for a few minutes before Dan and Gene returned, and Gary offered to show all of them around town.

He hoped he'd get some time alone with Scott during the afternoon, but it wasn't to be. Gary drove the guys all around town showing them the sights. They seemed to have a good time, but Scott was quiet—very quiet—which added to Gary's concern. In the early evening, they returned to Mark and Tyler's for dinner. Afterward Gary found himself alone with Scott in the family room. "I was going to ask if you ever heard any more from Frank."

"No." The question seemed to pull Scott out of his thoughts for a moment. "You were right; he seems to have backed off." Scott became quiet again, much to Gary's frustration, and he wasn't sure what to do. Then the others joined them and relieved the silence that was becoming uncomfortable.

Later Gary said his good-nights, and Scott pulled him aside. "I think I'm going to stay here tonight."

"Oh." Gary felt like he'd been punched in the stomach, but did his best to cover it. "I'll get your suitcase from the trunk." Feeling sort of dazed and confused, Gary retrieved the suitcase, handing it to Scott. "Good night." Gary didn't wait for Scott to answer. His decision already said plenty, and Gary didn't want the rejection he felt broadcast to everyone. Leaving Scott at the front door, he turned and walked toward his car.

"At least I know where I stand," he muttered to himself as he closed the car door, the last light of hope fading. The day had started so wonderfully. Gary started the car and pulled away from the house, wiping his eyes with the back of his hand as he drove toward his building.

Finding a place to park, he rode the elevator to his floor. He unlocked his door and let himself inside. Slipping off his coat, he went to his bedroom. He turned on a light and looked over at the still unmade bed. He could still almost see where Scott had lain that morning.

"He made his decision very plain." Gary knew that Scott was putting distance between them to make it easier when he had to go home. That much was clear to Gary. What hurt was that Scott had told him he loved him. "Goddamn it." Gary flopped down on the edge of the bed, holding his head in his hand, thinking, but no sparkling revelations came to mind. He got ready for bed and turned off the light. After all, he could at least *try* to sleep.

Chapter 18

SLEEP was the last thing that happened that night. For most of it, Gary stared at the ceiling wondering what he'd done wrong. He knew logically that he hadn't done anything, not really, but he felt empty. As the night wore on, his feelings of rejection and helplessness morphed into anger and frustration. He deserved an answer and a reason for being rejected, and he was bloody well going to get one. Finally, after hours of stewing, growling, and wondering, he finally fell asleep, only to have a soft tapping encroach on his consciousness.

Cracking his scratchy eyes open in the dim room, he heard the tapping again. It sounded like it was coming from his door. Getting up, he put on his robe and shuffled to the door, cracking it open to peer into the hallway. Scott stood in the middle of the hall, eyes down, hands behind his back, looking miserable. Gary stared, his eyes narrowing. Scott's body language spoke volumes—the stance, the eyes, and the slumped posture all screamed submissive insecurity. Opening the door, he saw Scott lift his eyes and let his hands fall to his sides.

"I'm sorry, Gary." Then the eyes lowered again, and Gary felt his anger and frustration slip away.

"Come on in." Gary stepped back, and a hunched-over Scott shuffled into the apartment. Gary closed the door, and Scott stopped in the middle of the room, wringing his hands. "Sit down and explain what happened. I thought we were so happy, and then after we visited Mark and Tyler you were so quiet. Then you didn't want to come back here with me."

Scott sat on the far side of the sofa, looking at Gary warily. "I needed to think about some things, and I tried all day, but whenever I did, I'd see you, or smell you, and then you'd touch me, and what I was thinking about would fly out of my head." Scott finally raised his face and looked Gary in the eye. "Tyler offered me a job yesterday, and I've been thinking about moving here." Gary saw Scott closely watching his expression. "But I kept asking myself what would happen if we didn't work out. But every time I thought about it, you were there, and I couldn't think straight."

"I thought you were putting some distance between us because you were leaving tomorrow and wanted to make it easier." Gary saw Scott's eyes soften into the same look that Mark had captured in the photograph while they were on vacation.

"That's what Dan said last night. I almost asked them to bring me back over here, but I needed to work things out." The hope Gary thought was dashed sprang back up.

"What did you decide?" Gary tried not to sound snippy, and he let Mark's advice play in his head. *It has to be Scott's decision.* "Are you leaving tomorrow?"

"Yes." This was like a roller coaster, and Gary felt the floor fall out from under him again. "I have to go so I can pack."

Gary felt a smile build on his face. "Are you saying you're going to move here?" he asked hesitantly.

Scott nodded, and Gary's smile broadened. "But I need to find my own place. I realized that if I move here, it can't be just for you; it has to be for me. I've spent my whole life in Pennsylvania, including the time I was in prison. After you left, I talked to Dan, and after he got done bawling me out for hurting you, he gave me some advice. He told me that maybe it was time for a change of scenery, a place where no one knew me or my past, a place to start over." Scott wiped his eyes. "And I figured he was right."

"Dan gives good advice." Gary could barely contain his excitement. Scott was going to move here. They could be together.

Scott's head shook slightly. "He also told me that I already had a place to go where someone loved me."

Gary slid along the sofa, not stopping until he was next to Scott. "Dan was right. You do." Gary slid his arms around Scott's waist, hugging him tightly as he tilted his head up toward Scott's. "I love you, Scott." Gary felt his eyes fill with happiness, and then Scott's lips met his, and all the worry, frustration, and rejection were forgotten. Scott was here with him, and he was going to stay with him. "Did you sleep last night?"

Scott shook his head. "Did you?"

"Not much." Gary stood up and opened his robe, letting it drop to the floor. He heard Scott's sudden intake of breath and the sound sent a shiver through him. Scott truly wanted him, desired him, and he felt like the sexiest man on earth. Strong arms wound around his waist, pulling him between Scott's long, thick legs. Lips latched onto one of his nipples, and Gary threw his head back as teeth gently scraped his skin, with Scott's tongue soothing right behind.

"You like that?" Gary saw the delight in his eyes as Scott took the other bud between his lips, giving it the same treatment as a pair of hot hands slid down Gary's back, cupping and exploring his butt.

"I think we'll be more comfortable in the bedroom," Gary moaned between panting breaths as Scott kept exploring his skin with his mouth.

Scott released Gary and stood up. Lifting him off his feet, he carried him toward the bedroom. "You're such a caveman sometimes," Gary giggled.

"You love it," Scott growled as he shifted to carry him through the door. Gary did love it. He hated it when Scott felt insecure and wished he could banish Scott's prison stance forever. A confident Scott was the sexiest thing on earth, and if that meant the occasional appearance of Caveman Scott, so be it. Gary bounced as Scott dropped him on the bed, laughing as he watched Scott's clothes disappear in a blur.

Scott prowled up the bed, looking like a panther stalking his prey, and Gary felt his cock throb as those feral-looking eyes locked onto his. Scott's tongue licked along his inner thigh and Gary moaned, spreading his legs farther apart. That magic tongue slid along his length and Gary whimpered, thrusting his hips forward.

"What do you want, Gary?" Scott repeated the motion, and Gary's ability to speak went with it. He tried, but all that came out were nonsense sounds.

"You," was the only sound he could make understood, and Scott leered at him as he kept lapping at his skin. Each stroke of that hot tongue sent Gary higher, and he loved it. The thought that he was going to have Scott in his bed, making love to him, in his life, on a regular basis, was the hottest thing he could imagine. That is, until Scott swirled his tongue around the head of Gary's cock. At that moment, Gary forgot his name and gripped the bedding in his fists.

"Love the way you taste," Scott mumbled as he licked again. Gary thrust his hips into the touch. "Relax, sweetheart."

Gary growled and bucked again. "How am I supposed to relax when you're doing that? It just isn't possible!" Gary could barely see straight, Scott's light touch driving him out of his mind. Scott's eyes gleamed as swallowed Gary down in one swift movement. Gary combed his fingers through the long, black hair, thrusting deep and hard. To his utter surprise and delight, Scott took everything he had and asked for more. "Love you," Gary murmured. He felt his vision blur as his climax overtook him, and he emptied himself down his lover's silken throat.

Gary gasped as Scott pulled off him, kissing him hard as strong knees pressed his legs apart. Gary lifted them, and fingers found his entrance, a long digit sliding inside him, finding his spot and making his eyes cross yet again. "God, you're good at that."

"What?" Scott asked innocently, as Gary felt that finger rub him deep inside again. "That?"

"Scott." Gary arched his body beneath Scott, his head slamming back against the pillow. "Don't play innocent—fuck me!"

The finger slipped away, and Scott got himself ready, his eyes gleaming down at Gary. "I love it when you talk dirty."

"Huh?" Gary had never really thought about it before. "You do?"

Scott positioned himself at Gary's entrance, holding still. "Fuck, yeah!" He didn't move, and Gary was becoming very impatient as his own arousal returned with a vengeance. "Tell me what you want, Gary."

"Fuck me through the mattress!" Gary cried out as Scott entered him in a single thrust, obviously taking Gary at his word. "Yeah! Do that again!"

Scott did. Pulling out, he thrust home, repeating the motion until Gary couldn't cry out any more, just whimper as he held on to Scott for dear life and rode his lover's passion and desire for all it was worth. "Love you, Scott."

"Love you too!" Scott drove himself home.

"Then show me! I won't break!"

Scott turned into a man possessed, driving deep and hard, hitting that perfect spot every single time. Gary's breath heaved as Scott took him to a place he'd never been before, one where they were joined completely. He could feel Scott's love and desire for him with each movement, and each flex of that powerful body. Scott's eyes were locked on his, wide open, forming a link that only increased their passion. Sweat beaded off their bodies, soaking the sheets and each other. "Can't last, Gary."

"Then come for me, Scott. Fill me, show me you love me!" Gary's second climax careened into him, stronger than the first, as Scott cried out in a low howl, both lost in the throes of orgasm. Scott collapsed forward onto Gary, gasping for breath as they held each other, neither able to move. Eventually Scott rolled off him, and Gary got up, grabbing a towel for a quick cleanup. They needed to talk about so many things. Gary climbed back into bed, and as Scott pulled him tightly to him, Gary closed his eyes just for a second. Scott's warmth enveloped him as strong hands lightly petted his skin. Hell, they could talk later. Scott spooned against Gary's back and kissed his neck softly, and Gary found himself nodding off. Talking was overrated anyway.

The heat behind him dissipated, and Gary cracked his eyes open, scooting backward to get warm again. "Where'd you go?" His question was met with a deep chuckle, and then the warmth was back, the bed dipping as Scott climbed back in against him. Gary rolled in Scott's embrace so he could face him. "You were amazing."

Scott rolled forward, pinning Gary beneath his broad body. "So were you." Scott captured his lips in a gentle kiss that left Gary's insides all melty and warm. "I hate to break the mood, but I think we may need to talk."

"You've changed your mind?" Gary tensed.

Scott's response was immediate. "No. But there are some things we need to discuss." He sounded so reasonable. "I can work for Tyler, but I need to find a place to live."

"You can stay here."

Scott shook his head. "I need a place of my own." Gary wasn't too happy about that. He'd been looking forward to having Scott in his bed. Scott began to laugh. "No pouting," he said.

Gary pulled in his lower lip. "Then how about a compromise? We could get a bigger place here in the building. They'll let me transfer my lease to a larger unit. We could get one with two bedrooms. That way you'll have your own space." Gary let his hands slink around Scott's neck as he kissed him. "Is that a yes?"

"That's an 'I'll think about it'." Scott smiled, and Gary ran his hands along the big man's ribs. "That's not fair." He squealed and tried to get away.

"You'll think about it." Gary came after him, and Scott tried to get off the bed, landing on the floor with a thump. Gary peered over the edge of the mattress before sliding down on top of Scott, wiggling his fingers in the air as they both laughed. Scott grabbed Gary's wrists to hold off his tormenting fingers and brought their lips together. "Give up yet?"

"I'll think about it." They both broke into fits of laughter. "Can we be serious for a minute?" Scott's laughter faded away, and Gary's went along with it. "I really need to move here for me, you know? I love you, Gary, but I can't move here for you. I have to be independent. Besides, what if you find out that I snore like a lumberjack and can't stand to live with me?"

Gary smirked down at Scott still beneath him on the floor. "I already know you don't snore, and we practically lived together on the ship."

"That's just it. The ship was vacation; what if it wasn't real?"

"Does this feel real to you?" Gary leaned forward and kissed Scott hard, pulling on those full lips with his own. Scott nodded slowly when Gary broke the kiss. "It does to me too. If you want your own apartment, I can live with that, but think how nice it'll be to have me close at hand." Gary reached behind him, running his hand along Scott's length, feeling it firm in his hand. "Imaging how much fun it'll be having my hands so close by." Gary grinned down at Scott as he kept stroking.

"I can see the benefits of that," Scott said.

Gary stroked again and then pulled his hand away. "I'm serious, Scott. I'd love to have you live with me. But I want you to be comfortable, and I'm just happy that you're going to be here. I know you need to be independent, but can't you be independent with me?"

Gary saw Scott's eyes start to water, and then he was pulling Gary down, hugging him close. Scott didn't say anything, just held him, and Gary wasn't sure if he was upset, happy, or trying to comfort him from some imagined disappointment. "That you want me is so wonderful." Gary felt himself relax and went with Scott's happiness. When he'd opened that door and seen Scott's prison stance, he'd felt so bad. He loved Scott like this: happy.

"Love you, Scott. I'll always want you." Gary felt Scott's hands slide over his skin, and even though they'd already made love twice, he could feel Scott getting him excited again.

"No one's ever made me feel the way you do."

Gary lifted his head. "No one?"

"No. I've had people who said they loved me, but no one had ever made me feel like this."

"Like what, Scott?" Gary swallowed around the lump in his throat. "Please tell me."

"Like I'm the most important person in the world." Gary felt Scott's lips travel over his. "Like no one else matters but me."

"Scott, you are the most important person in my world. That's part of being in love. You get to make someone else feel like they're the center of your world." Scott kissed him again, and Gary snuggled against his hot skin right there on the floor.

"I'm sorry I hurt you and...."

Gary put a finger over Scott's lips to quiet him.

"You're here now, and that's all that counts."

Chapter 19

"Is Scott coming back soon?" Mark asked as he slipped off his stool.

"He called this morning as he was just starting his drive out." The last two weeks had been blessedly hectic both with clients and with preparing for his first Christmas with Scott. He'd scheduled himself in the far reaches of his territory. The trips to Green Bay and Lacrosse had been long but productive, and had helped keep his excited mind off Scott's absence. Every time his phone rang, he found himself dreading that it was Scott calling to say he'd changed his mind.

"You have to be really excited." Mark led the way out of his studio and through the back door to the antique store, with Gary following behind. The store was quiet, so Mark took a seat on one of the sofas in the back of the store and motioned for Gary to sit as well. "So tell me why you look so terrified."

Gary knew he was probably going to sound stupid, but he had to talk to someone, and he knew Mark would listen. "For the last two weeks, I've been scared Scott would change his mind. And now that he's on his way, I'm afraid that I may have pressured him into moving in with me." Gary began wringing his hands in his lap. "How long did you know Tyler before you moved in with him?"

"Just a few days actually. My mother threw me out when she found out I was gay, and Tyler took me in. We've been together ever since." Gary saw Mark smile as he went down memory lane for a few seconds. "The thing I want you to know is that it wasn't perfect for Tyler and me. We had to get used to each other and learn to live together. We knew we loved each other quickly, just like you and Scott, but the hard part was learning to forgive each other's failings. We also needed to learn to give each other space." Mark looked around the store as the front bell rang, and Gary saw Tyler greet customers before returning to his desk.

"I guess what's got me concerned is... what if he's not happy?"

Mark began to laugh. "Gary, did you hear yourself? You didn't say what if *you're* not happy, but what if *Scott's* not happy. You're worried about him, and there's a surefire way to find out." Gary was all ears. "Ask him. I know it sounds simple, but talking to one another, even about things that make either of you uncomfortable, helps... a lot." They got up so a customer wandering through the store could see the sofa, and then sat back down as the customer moved on. "Will you need help moving his things in?"

Gary shook his head. "Scott said that he got everything in the back of his truck, so there can't be very much. I've got all my stuff moved to the new apartment, and his room is clean and ready for him."

"If you and Scott are anything like Tyler and me, he won't use it."

"I hope not." One of the things Gary was looking forward to most was having Scott sleeping next to him every night. Gary's phone rang, and he smiled when he saw it was Scott.

"How's the trip?"

"I'm in Indiana, so I'll be there at dinnertime if the traffic in Chicago isn't too bad." He could hear the excitement in Scott's voice, and that went a long way toward helping to allay his fears.

"Call me when you get close, and I'll give you directions to the building."

"I'm good. Dan got me detailed directions from the Internet. I'll call when I get closer."

"Okay, can't wait to see you." Gary was so ready to see his lover again. He turned away from Mark. "Can't wait for you to see our new place and try out our bed."

"I like the sound of that." Scott's voice became deep and throaty, the rumbling going right through him. Gary swallowed and said good-bye before he embarrassed himself in the store.

"I take it that was Scott," Mark snickered as Gary put his phone away, trying to discreetly adjust himself, but obviously he wasn't discreet enough.

"He'll be here early this evening." Gary checked his watch. "The man must have been up at the crack of dawn."

Mark smiled. "I have to get back to work, or I'll never get done." They got up and Mark gave him a hug before disappearing into his studio, and Gary went up front to talk to Tyler.

They talked business and shared a little gossip. Gary left the store with a big order and spent the rest of the afternoon visiting other clients in the area. Business was good and getting better. For that, he was exceedingly grateful. The new apartment was more expensive, and while Scott had a job with Tyler, Gary wanted to be able to handle the rent on his own if he had to. Gary knew Scott wanted to be independent and had insisted on paying his way, including chipping in for half of the increased security deposit, but Gary wanted Scott to have breathing room if he needed it.

Leaving his last client, he drove home and rode the elevator to one of the floors near the top of the building. Not only had they gotten a larger apartment, they'd also gotten a great view of the city. After changing his clothes, Gary began making dinner as he waited for Scott to call so he could meet him downstairs and help him unload the truck.

The sunlight dimmed through the windows, and Scott hadn't called. Darkness settled and Gary turned on the lights, but still no call. Gary tried Scott's cell phone, but got no answer. He began pacing the floor. Reluctantly, he sat in front of the television and ate dinner, watching the news, but there didn't seem to be traffic troubles. He even went on the Internet for Chicago traffic information, but everything he could find told him that traffic was moving relatively smoothly, particularly along Scott's route. With each passing hour, Gary's worries multiplied.

Gary jumped as the phone in his pocket vibrated. He scrunched his brow when he saw a strange number in Scott's area code. "Hello," he said quizzically.

"Gary? It's Dan." He sounded agitated and worried.

"What's happened? Has Scott called you?"

"Yeah. I just hung up with him. He got pulled over in Illinois near the border and the state trooper's giving him a hard time." Gary jumped to his feet and began pacing. "He said he'd been sitting by the side of the road for a while, and he's getting nervous."

"Call him and tell him I'm on my way."

"Gary, he's afraid they're going to take him to jail."

He was already pulling on his coat. "I'm on my way." Gary hung up and frantically began dialing. "Sam? It's Gary."

"Hey, what's going on?" Gary relayed what little he knew about Scott. "I'm nearby. Meet me in front of your building." Sam hung up, and Gary hurried, rushing to get ready and pulling the door closed behind him, hurrying to the elevator. Watching the dial, it wasn't moving and Gary became impatient. Hurrying down the hall, he pushed open the door to the stairwell and began his trek to the ground.

Banging the doors as he rushed outside, he saw a police car out front with Sam's head hanging out. "Hurry and get in." Gary rushed to the passenger door and slammed the door shut as Sam flipped on the lights and took off. When they got to the freeway, Gary began dialing Scott's number.

"Answer, come on, pick up," he murmured to nothing.

"Gary?" He could hear the worry in Scott's voice.

"I'm on my way with Sam."

"They want me to leave the truck and go with them. They said they'll have the truck towed, but it's got all my stuff in it." Scott was sounding plaintive and scared. "I don't know what to do."

Gary held on as Sam flew down the freeway. "We'll be there soon. Do you have the papers they gave you when you were released?"

"Yeah. I showed them to the officer, but he said I had to go with him anyway." Gary saw Sam reach over, and he handed him the phone.

"Scott, did he say why he pulled you over." Sam listened for a few seconds. "That's a joke." He listened some more. "He's coming back to your door? Good, hand him the phone." Sam continued driving like a bat out of hell, the phone against his ear.

"This is Sam Davis of the Milwaukee Police Department. What did Scott do?" Gary hung on as Sam listened. "I'm on my way, and my next call is to the FBI." Sam turned briefly to Gary and winked. "Scott was proven innocent, and those papers are real. I'm five minutes away!" Sam tossed the phone back at Gary and the car picked up more speed. "Stubborn stupid son of a bitch."

The Illinois border passed in a whirl, and they saw flashing lights and Scott's truck on the other side. Without turning off his lights, Sam pulled into a pass through and pulled up behind the police car. "Stay here, Gary."

Sam got out of the car and walked toward the police car, hands clearly visible. A second police car joined them, and Gary watched through the window as Sam talked to the other two officers. He could see them blustering back and forth until the second officer stepped back shaking his head before going back to his car, turning off the lights and leaving the scene.

Gary watched as Sam returned to the car and got in. "I suggest you join Scott in his truck." Sam smiled brightly, and Gary moved toward him, bouncing back against the seatbelt in his haste. "I'll follow you home." With a laugh, Gary unfastened it and gave Sam a hug before leaving the warm car and rushing to Scott's truck. He pulled open the heavy door and climbed inside.

Scott turned toward him and smiled a little before putting the truck in gear. "Sam said he'd follow us." Scott nodded, but didn't say anything as he pulled out into traffic. Gary turned around and saw Sam's lights go out as he fell in behind them.

"Are you okay Scott? Why didn't you call me?"

"I…." Gary saw Scott's hands practically turn white as he gripped the wheel. "I just need to drive."

"Okay." Gary sat back, but kept looking at Scott. His face was set, but his eyes looked drawn. He knew that if Scott weren't driving, he'd be standing in that damn, horrible prison stance, trying to seem as unobtrusive as possible.

The trip down had seemed like a blur, but the trip back seemed to take forever, with Scott not saying two words the entire time. Gary guided him through town and to the building, helping him find a parking space.

It was well past dark when they got out of the truck and walked to the front door. Sean was waiting for them inside the lobby. "Tom and Bill are on their way, and Bobby should be here any second."

"I don't have that much," Scott murmured. Gary saw him standing near the truck, watching over his things.

Sean went around back and lowered the tailgate. "It's dark, cold, and everything has to go up fifteen floors." Sean began taking out boxes and carrying them inside, with Gary and Sam right behind him. Scott stayed by the truck and continued unloading.

The others arrived and together they made short work of the job. Scott, Sean, and Bobby got things unloaded and into the elevator. Gary, Tom, and Bill got things out of the elevator and into the apartment. When the last of it was carried in, Gary ushered Scott into their new apartment. Gary made a pot of hot chocolate, and they all warmed themselves before saying their good-byes.

Gary watched as Scott talked to Sam. Scott put out his hand, and Sam pulled him into a hug before he and Sean waved good-night and left the apartment, with the rest of their friends right behind them. Gary waved a final good-night as the elevator door opened, and then he shut the door.

Turning around, what he saw made him want to yell. Scott was standing in the kitchen doorway with his head down, and Gary wanted to scream at the police officer who had given him such a hard time. Sam had told him that the officer had stopped Scott because he was going a little fast, and when he ran his license, the rookie saw Scott's release from prison, and there was a be-on-the-lookout for a rapist, so he figured he had his man even though he didn't read the bulletin clearly and Scott didn't match the suspect's description. He just figured he'd get a career boost if he captured a fugitive. The arrival of the other officer along with Sam had helped the overzealous rookie see reason.

Gary walked to Scott and took his hand, running his thumb over the knuckles. "Let's sit down." Without waiting for a response, he tugged Scott to the sofa. Gary sat next to him, running a hand along Scott's arm. "Why didn't you call me?"

Scott finally lifted his eyes from the floor. "I was ashamed."

Gary tried to wait patiently for Scott even as he felt anger boiling inside.

"What kind of life can you have with me? I'll never be left alone, and they'll make you pay for being with me. On the ship, you were the one Frank shoved in the closet, and it was you who had to come get me tonight."

Gary felt his anger with the officer slip away as more immediate things took precedence. Without thinking, he scooted closer. "If it means having you with me, sharing my bed and my life, I'll risk being pushed in the closet and the occasional rush to the border. That doesn't matter. What does matter is that you have me, and we have friends." Gary lifted Scott's chin slightly, pulling his eyes off the floor. "Good friends who'll help us move you in on the coldest night of the year so far."

"But what if I'm not worth it?" Gary thought he could feel his heart hurt at the plaintive tone in Scott's voice.

"You are worth it to me." Gary brought his lips to Scott's, letting his arms wrap around his neck. "More than worth it." He felt Scott respond and then rest his head against Gary's shoulder.

"Would you like to see your new home?"

Scott nodded and lifted his head, standing up and pulling Gary to his feet.

"This is the living room, obviously."

Scott looked around, taking it all in. "I love the floors."

"Me too." They were polished parquet and the room had opulent crown moldings and beautiful window frames in richly finished wood. "The building used to be a residence hotel in the twenties and was quite expensive." He led Scott by the hand, wanting to maintain reassuring contact with his lover. "This is the dining room." It was good-sized—not huge, but a luxury in an apartment. "The kitchen's small, but efficient." Gary walked him through and then back to the living room. "I had the guys put most of your things in your room." Gary led him to the bedroom and opened the door. There were boxes stacked against the walls, and a bed, dresser, and a few pieces of miscellaneous furniture. "I had your chair put in the living room."

Gary saw Scott look at him and smile, really smile for the first time since he'd arrived. "This is mine?"

"Yes. Your own private domain," Gary said as Scott walked into the room. "Are you hungry?" Scott nodded, and Gary left him alone, going to the kitchen to heat him some dinner. He could hear Scott moving things around and the occasional bang of furniture against the floor. When the food was ready, Gary walked to Scott's room. The bed was assembled and made, with a large open box sitting near the foot.

"Dinner's ready."

Scott finished putting his pillows on the bed and followed Gary to the table.

"I'll be right back," Gary said.

When Gary returned, Scott had finished his food and looked sort of drowsy. "I'm going to turn in if that's okay." Scott got up, and he felt Scott's lips against his, lightly kissing him. Gary watched as Scott walked down the hall and into his room.

Gary put the dishes in the sink before following Scott down the hall. Peeking in his lover's room, he saw him getting ready for bed. "I have one more thing to show you."

"Okay." Scott finished pulling on his T-shirt, and Gary took his hand, leading him across the hall. "Is this your room?"

"No, Scott. This is our room." Gary felt him stiffen in the doorway. "This is the room I hope you'll share with me." Gary led him inside. The room was dark, with only a bedside lamp and a fire burning in the fireplace providing light. The queen-size bed was turned down, waiting for them. Gary turned to Scott and saw his eyes scan the room and stop at the dresser. Gary had framed some of the pictures of the two of them, and Scott picked one up, examining it.

"You mean it." Scott set the picture back on the dresser, turning to look at Gary.

Gary stepped to Scott slowly, his arms slinking around Scott's narrow waist, looking into his eyes. "Yes, I mean it. You're not my roommate—you're my lover. The man I want to go to sleep next to and the one I want to see when I wake up." Gary used a few stray hairs as an excuse to glide his fingers through Scott's silky mane.

"What did I ever do to deserve you?" Scott's lip began to tremble ever so slightly.

"The same thing I did to deserve you." Gary swallowed the lump in his throat and brought Scott's lips to his.

"Sometimes I think I died and went to heaven." Scott returned Gary's kiss as he guided them toward the bed. Between kisses, Gary tugged Scott's shirt over his head, then his own, and they stepped out of their pants when they pooled at their feet. They tumbled naked onto the bed, skin to skin. "This has to be heaven."

Gary lifted Scott's head as he nibbled on the base of Scott's neck. "This is better than heaven. This is home, our home." Then Scott kissed him and so much more.

Chapter 20

GARY woke happily after a tumultuous night. Scott had had a nightmare, rousing him in the middle of the night, thrashing and then screaming. Gary had done his best to wake him in as soothing a way as possible. Once Scott was comfortable again, Gary had held him close until he stopped shaking, then he felt Scott kissing him, hard and needy, and Gary gave everything he had. Their lovemaking was fast, furious, and wore both of them out. Then Scott fell back to sleep and didn't move for the rest of the night.

When Gary woke, he saw Scott's sleeping face, long black hair covering the pillow, and a tattooed shoulder peeking out from under the covers. He knew he shouldn't, but he just couldn't resist. Gary's fingers traced the outlines of Scott's ink, the smooth skin making his fingers tingle. He saw those big brown eyes flutter open and a smile cross Scott's face.

"Morning," the big sleepy man mumbled as he pulled Gary closer.

"Merry Christmas Eve." Gary smiled against Scott's lips before giving him a quick kiss. "What is that beeping?" A soft electronic tone emanated from the living room and then stopped.

"I think that's my phone, it's been doing that for the last few days, and I don't know why." One of the things Gary had found out in the last few weeks was that Scott was a complete technophobe.

Gary hopped out of the bed and found the phone, returning with it and jumping back into bed, purposely crawling over Scott in the process before settling on the bed and opening the phone. "You have a message." Gary showed Scott the display. "That's what the yellow envelope means.

"Would you get it?" Scott looked lost.

Gary shook his head and pressed the voice mail button, entered Scott's code, and listened. "Mr. Haworth, this is Jonathon Cooper with CNN. We're doing a story on people released from prison who were wrongly accused. We'd like to interview you to find out how you're adjusting and the challenges you're facing. Please call me at...." Gary was stunned and looked over at Scott without saying anything. Instead he pressed the replay button and handed the phone to Scott.

He saw Scott's eyes widen in surprise, and then Scott shook his head and closed the phone. "Should I do it?" He sounded frightened.

"If you want to. It's a chance to tell your side of the story and maybe help someone else." Gary slid under the covers, wrapping his arms around Scott's chest. "You don't have to decide now. Besides, it's Christmas, and we have more important, fun things to do."

"Like what?" Scott cuddled next to Gary, their warmth mingling in the bed.

"There's that." Gary felt Scott's roaming hands. "And we have a party that Fabrizio, one of my clients, invited us to. Mark and Tyler also invited us to their house for the evening, and tomorrow we're joining Sean and Sam for Christmas dinner."

"Is Fabrizio the guy you told me about?" Scott's hands stopped moving, cupping Gary's butt.

"Yes, and he really wants to meet you."

"Okay, but if he pats this," Scott said, squeezing Gary's nether cheeks, "he won't have arms left." As Scott pinned him between the mattress and his muscular body, Gary felt a surge of desire that he had to quell, or else they'd never get out of the apartment.

"Going all caveman, I see." Gary loved it.

Scott growled deep in his throat. "I just don't share well."

"Me, neither." Gary leaned up to kiss Scott and found himself on the receiving end of a lip lock that stole his breath away. Giving up thoughts of anything else, he let his caveman have his decadent way twice, once in bed and a second time in the shower before they finally managed to get dressed. "You sure know how to say Merry Christmas." Gary got another kiss as he pulled on his coat.

Scott's eyes danced with mischief. "That was just the warm up. It's not even Christmas yet." Damn, the man's deep and rumbly voice could get him going fast. Gary actually gauged how close the sofa was before Scott got his coat, but let his ardor cool for the time being. That didn't last long, though, because as soon as the elevator door closed, Scott had him pressed against the wall, kissing the air from his lungs.

Somehow they made it to the car and through town to Fabrizio's studio. The party had already started and, as soon as they entered, Gary was encased in a hug from the designer.

"Merry Christmas." He heard Scott's growl and obviously Fabrizio did as well, because his hands remained north of the equator.

"Is this Scott?" the designer gushed as he approached Scott and engulfed him in a hug as well. Then he showed them around and made introductions. Scott appeared famished and went directly for the food.

Gary handed Fabrizio a small decorative box with a bow on it. "Merry Christmas."

The designer grinned and opened the box, smiling as he looked at what was inside. "Is this sea glass?"

"Yes, I found them on St. Croix."

Fabrizio grinned. "I have just the thing for them. Thank you." The smile widened, and Gary was pleased the designer was happy. Fabrizio excused himself as he was called away and walked toward the back to handle the crisis. Gary let his attention shift to Scott making his way through the nibbles.

"He's yummy." Fabrizio appeared back at Gary's elbow and handed him a drink. "It's noon somewhere." Fabrizio clinked their glasses together before sipping the pink concoction. "Rumor has it he's an ex-con."

Gary set the glass on a nearby table. "He spent eight years in prison for something he didn't do, and was proven innocent and released." Gary didn't try to hide the edge in his voice. "You'd think people would want to help instead of expecting the worst."

"I think he's a doll." Fabrizio motioned to where Scott was talking to one of the ladies. "Gayle is a great designer, but a primo bitch when it comes to people, and look, he's got her eating out of his hand." Gary saw the two of them talking animatedly and smiling at each other. Then Scott unbuttoned his shirt, showing her his tattoo and she unbuttoned her top a bit, slipping it off a shoulder.

Gary laughed. "They're comparing ink." Fabrizio moved on to talk to other guests and Gary stood off to one side, watching his lover. He'd come so far in such a short time. He was actually at a party and talking to people, and to top things off, he hadn't seen "the stance" in a whole week. Other people joined Scott's conversation, and he kept smiling at them. Gary saw one of the women appear to ask him something and then touch his arm. Usually Scott would flinch, but this time he turned and smiled at Gary, a big smile that said "I'm okay, having a good time, and love you," all at once. Gary wandered over and joined the conversation, Scott's arm snaking around his waist.

The party wound down in the early afternoon, and they headed home. In the apartment Gary plugged in the Christmas tree, and they snuggled together. "Where did all those presents come from?" Scott asked, pulling Gary closer.

Gary angled his head to look at Scott. "Some of them arrived a few days ago from Dan and Gene, but most of them are from me." Gary smiled at the look of wonder on Scott's face. "I figured you deserved a special Christmas since you missed so many."

"It's already special—I got you." Scott kissed him. Gary shifted on the sofa, and Scott's embrace tightened. Gary reached over to the coffee table and used the remote to turn on the stereo, and warm Christmas music filled the quiet room. They spent most of the afternoon like that, just being together. "When do we have to leave?"

Gary had almost dozed off, he was so comfortable. "In about an hour." Reluctantly, he got up. "I promised Tyler I'd make some caramel corn."

"Doesn't that take a long time?"

"I have a microwave recipe, so it only takes fifteen minutes."

"Then I'll go down and get the mail." Gary heard the door close and began popping the corn while he made up the caramel mixture. By the time Scott returned, the buttery mixture was coming out.

"Would you like to try some?"

No answer.

"Scott?" Gary put caramel corn out to cool and peeked around the corner. Scott was sitting on the sofa, a letter in his hand. "What is it?"

Scott finished reading and handed the paper to Gary.

> Dear Scott,
>
> What happened on the ship woke me up, and I decided I needed to get some help. When I got home, I contacted a grief counselor and she's been helping me a lot. I'm writing this letter because she says I need to resolve my issues with you in order to move on.
>
> It's been very hard for me to let go of the way I blamed you for my sister's death. She was the most important person in my life, the only person who loved me, and now she's gone. I now realize that I blamed you instead of dealing with my own grief. I also realize that you never hurt

her and weren't responsible for the attack and aren't responsible for her death.

I hope that someday you can find it in your heart to forgive me for all the grief I caused you. With my therapist's help, I've come to realize that you're a victim as much as my sister was.

I sincerely hope that from here on out, your life is full and rich.

Frank Garrett

Gary looked up from the letter and saw Scott staring up at him. Gary handed the handwritten piece of notebook paper back to Scott, who folded it and put it back in the envelope as a tear ran down his strong face.

"I never thought...."

Gary sat next to him, holding his hand, letting Scott express something that appeared to be quite difficult for him.

"That bastard who hurt that girl, he turned us all into victims: me, her, Frank, her parents, all of us." A second tear followed the first. "I think I'll call CNN and tell them I'll do the interview. Maybe it's time I stopped being a victim."

Gary felt so happy and proud he thought he was going to burst. "I'll go with you if you want."

Scott blinked away the moisture from his eyes as he nodded. "I'd like that." Scott stood up, pulling Gary into his strong arms. "I'd like that a lot." They stood together hugging until it was time to leave for Tyler and Mark's party.

"Feel better?" Gary asked as Scott released him.

"Yeah, but I can't describe it." Gary felt Scott's lips ghost over his. "We should go." They got their coats, and Gary packed the gifts he'd gotten for Mark and Tyler before leaving the apartment and walking with Scott to the elevator.

Scott couldn't describe what he was feeling, but Gary could. Sean always talked about looking for that special wine, the one that only cost ten bucks but tastes like so much more. He called it looking for the unexpected vintage. That's what Gary felt like he'd found in Scott—the most special, wonderful—and unexpected vintage—ever.

ANDREW GREY grew up in western Michigan with a father who loved to tell stories and a mother who loved to read them. Since then he has lived throughout the country and traveled throughout the world. He has a master's degree from the University of Wisconsin-Milwaukee and works in information systems for a large corporation. Andrew's hobbies include collecting antiques, gardening, and leaving his dirty dishes anywhere but in the sink (particularly when writing). He considers himself blessed with an accepting family, fantastic friends, and the world's most supportive and loving partner. Andrew currently lives in beautiful historic Carlisle, Pennsylvania.

Visit Andrew's web site at http://www.andrewgreybooks.com and blog at http://andrewgreybooks.livejournal.com/. E-mail him at andrewgrey@comcast.net.

Contemporary Romance by ANDREW GREY

http://www.dreamspinnerpress.com

Also by ANDREW GREY

http://www.dreamspinnerpress.com

Contemporary Fantasy by ANDREW GREY